Crannóg 56 spring 2022

Editorial Board

Sandra Bunting
Ger Burke
Jarlath Fahy
Tony O'Dwyer

ISSN 1649-4865
ISBN 978-1-907017-62-9

Cover image: *Flora, by Pamela Sztybel*
Cover image sourced by Sandra Bunting
Cover design by Wordsonthestreet
Published by Wordsonthestreet for Crannóg magazine @CrannogM
www.wordsonthestreet.com@wordsstreet

CONTENTS

Submissions for Crannóg 57 open May 1st until May 31st
Publication date is September 30th 2022

Crannóg is published bi-annually in spring and autumn.

Submission Times:
Month of November for spring issue.
Month of May for autumn issue.

We will <u>not read</u> submissions sent outside these times.

POETRY:
Send no more than three poems. Each poem should be under 50 lines.
PROSE:
Send one story. Stories should be under 2,000 words.

We do not accept postal submissions.
When emailing your submission we require three things:

1. *The text of your submission included both in body of email and as a Word attachment (this is to ensure correct layout. We may, however, change your layout to suit our publication).*
2. *A brief bio in the third person. Include this both in body and in attachment.*
3. *A postal address for contributor's copy in the event of publication.*

For full submission details, to learn more about Crannóg Magazine, to purchase copies of the current issue, or take out a subscription, log on to our website:

www.crannogmagazine.com

The Healer

Aoibheann McCann

PATRICIA IS SKYPING MARY. Mary's fiancé, Mateo, appears now and then to announce his presence by waving at the screen. He laughs when they start talking about travelling to Abadiânia from the coast by train. He leans his head in over the keyboard to emphasise that there isn't exactly a network of trains on his continent and suggests that they go to Cancun instead.

Patricia skypes Mary again later, ready with jokes about conquistadores, aimed at Mateo and his pale brown skin. She refers to the fact that the Irish helped his country break free of the colonial yoke. He announces his departure from the room loudly. They agree on dates and then hang up to book the flights.

A month later Mary tells Patricia she is pregnant. Patricia feels the sucker punch in the gut but smiles and mimes the congratulations dance she has become so good at. Patricia offers to let her back out of the trip but Mary has to cross the border every three months because of her visa, Latino fiancé or no. They arrange to meet at the airport.

Patricia flies out the day after the big conference in work. She tells them all laughingly that she is going there for plastic surgery. After the second flight, Patricia has an all-day stopover in Rio. She wants to see Christ the Redeemer but imagines a taxi driver might drive her into a favela and have her killed. Through the high windows of the airport she sees the dry hills that surround the city. The only sightseeing she does is of the local women, their impossible curves sculpted perfectly into their tight clothes.

They drive from Brasilia airport in the early light. Through the tinted glass windows of the black sedan, that comes with a driver, they see brown grilled shutters pulled down around every building. Mary says it is the same in Santiago where she lives, four thousand miles away. Everywhere in this capital city, cut out of the jungle in a 1950s resurgence of colonialism, there are billboards with sketches of the luxury apartments that will be built. When they work out the price in euros, they are not as cheap as they expect. On the motorway, they pass bleak empty buildings, gutted and sprayed with ominous graffiti. They do not cross any railway lines; they do not see any jungle.

The main street in the village is made of red dirt. The pousada is down a smaller dirt road off the main street. A teenage security guard comes out to greet them from a shack by the Fleur de Lis iron gate. His t-shirt says Filthy Stinking Rich, Well, Two out of Three ain't Bad. He asks the driver to make them translate the t-shirt's message when he sees them stare. When they explain, he laughs uproariously and reveals two missing front teeth.

The door to their room is made of corrugated steel and opens in from a courtyard. There are two narrow wooden beds under the iron bars of the window. After lunch on the porch, the owner, a white-haired American woman, says that a local woman does manicures and it would be good for them to support her. Patricia did three languages for her Leaving Cert so she tries to converse with the manicurist, but the woman is making slicing motions across her throat between coats of nail varnish. Patricia thinks she is saying that several women have been murdered here, in this very pousada. She is alarmed, so doesn't try to contradict the white daisies she is painting on her toes, though she thinks they are tacky. When she tells Mary about the garbled conversation, Mary touches her belly in alarm.

When the rain comes down it is warm and heavy and floods the street. Ducks, ducklings, dogs, puppies and small children appear. When the sun comes back and bakes it all to red again, Patricia and Mary go for a walk. They see houses with no windows and no doors, there is a woman with a baby on her back going through the bins, there is a family living in a garage. The poverty proliferates the further away from the pousada they go, as do the sports bars, and the small menacing men glaring out from under their baseball caps. It is all too much for them and their European guilt, so they turn back. They buy two of the crude heart-shaped windchimes made of copper and dirty unpolished crystals that are hanging across the door of the garage. The kids grin as they watch their father twist copper wire with pliers, reshape it into free rings to go with the purchases. They buy fake designer flipflops in a shop like a shed. They buy hammocks to bring home that they will never put up. The rings turn their fingers green by nightfall.

In the evening there is an eighties film they have never heard of in the courtyard of the juice bar. The electricity goes, shutting down the film and the streetlights, enveloping them in a darkness full of the sound of crickets. Patricia looks around to see if anyone is going to do anything but people just wait quietly, listening to the screaming insects, until it comes back on.

On Saturday, the locals open the boots of their cars which contain huge speaker systems. Reggaetón blasts out and they dance on the red roads. The armed police stand watching, with guns and truncheons strapped to their belts. Patricia doesn't try to talk to the locals after the experience with the manicurist. Instead they sit in the juice bar and talk to the new arrivals from Europe and the US, people with wigs or bald heads, people in wheelchairs, people on crutches. There is a gift shop that sells new age books, crystals and religious paraphernalia. They buy pink crystal rosary beads and wear them around their neck like everyone else.

When Mary falls asleep early, Patricia goes back to the juice bar alone. She gets locked in the toilet until a woman from Cork, who tells her voluntarily that she is allergic to everything chemical, gets her out. Patricia asks her if she has ever seen the Healer do physical operations. She says she hasn't except on YouTube and even then, she couldn't watch it through. A German guy at the table next to them says he happened upon one the last time he was here, that he saw a woman sliced open with a pair of nail scissors, a yellow lump pulled out of her back. He says she was in a trance, that she did not scream or seem to feel any pain.

There is a man with Lyme disease staying at the pousada, he is from San Francisco, his whole bedside locker is covered in pill bottles, he cannot stop shaking. He has been here twice before and buys them green coconuts punched open with straws sticking out. They lie in the hammocks under the mango trees and talk about the other guests. The two young Australian guys who are covered in tattoos and piercings, with stretchers in their ears. They are junkies looking for a cure, an end to the rollercoaster of on-off addiction, an end to the cycle of rehab, partying, rehab. The couple with dreadlocks who wear clothes decorated with small mirrors and bright braiding. They have a small dirty toddler who wanders around the enclosed courtyard with only a shrunken t-shirt on, while her parents Skype her maternal grandfather loudly asking for money for a flight to Peru, so they can do an ayahuasca ritual in the jungle. The kitchen staff stare at the half-naked child and mutter about white people and how they bring up their children. Patricia tries to explain in her mixture of French and Spanish that they are the exception not the rule but the women shake their heads and get back to the cooking.

The guests share an early dinner of salads and pinto beans on the porch, hummingbirds drink from the gladioli as they eat. The Australian guys say that after an AA meeting the night before, they saw green and red streaks of light rising above the centre like laser ladders to the sky. The landlady has framed pictures of a similar phenomenon. Though there are no shops that sell anything other than sweets or gifts, there are pharmacies everywhere. White, clean pharmacies that develop the photos at western prices, photos that prove that there are unseen orbs of light everywhere in the village.

Everyone assumes Patricia has cancer. She doesn't contradict them. When the other guests ask Mary why she is there, she smiles and touches her stomach. She is serene, Madonna like. She is showing already and crocheting a purple and green blanket for the baby. Patricia wants to be happy for her but she has tried Clomid, Glucophage, Naltrexone, Tamoxifen and has had a laparoscopy. She has had trans-vaginal ultrasounds, been examined inside and out, had phials and phials of blood taken from the crook of her elbow but nothing seems to be wrong. She has tried two rounds of IVF though she has balked at surrogacy or adoption. She has gone to a homeopath, an acupuncturist, a reiki healer, a Mayan masseuse and has joined a mindfulness class.

On Monday morning they dress in white because that is the rule here. They go to the centre twice that day, and again on Tuesday and Wednesday. From the outside it looks like a barn. Before they go in they write down why they are here on small pieces of white paper, and it is translated for them to pass to the Healer. They are only permitted to sit in the antechamber because they are new. They are surrounded by statues of the Black Madonna, pink and white lumps of crystal, and big bunches of flowers, mostly pink roses. Julie Andrews sings 'Edelweiss' through the speakers. They cannot cross their legs or arms and must sit still for hours on the wooden church pews with their eyes closed. A fat blonde woman pokes them with a long ruler if they transgress. When the meditation reaches a steady pulse, they line up to walk past the car dealer, who is a Healer three days a week, who incarnates into various saints and doctors from the past so that he can perform miracles. He is surrounded by men and women in white who stand by his ornate wooden throne guarding him. His eyes change colour every time they pass. Sometimes he nods at a woman in the line and she is taken by the arm through a door behind the throne. Patricia imagines him ripping out her ovaries with a blunt scalpel or cutting off her breasts with a rusty saw.

In between the meditation days, they drink juice, or lie in the hammocks sweating. They go to the waterfall, a single stream pouring over a boulder just over head height. They go there with the permission from the Healer, a scribble in pencil written on one of the small white scraps of paper. On the long hot path, the red earth shines with specks of crystal, they see geckos, and pink, yellow and green spotted butterflies. Patricia stands under the water in her togs and feels the water wash away all her cynicism and bitchiness. It is easy to believe anything here. A huge blue amorphous butterfly flaps across the forest path as she waits for Mary to finish her turn.

When she next walks down the line at the centre Patricia cries like she has never cried before, a racking all-body sobbing, but after she feels a white calm. Patricia changes the message on her scrap of paper, she wants to feel like this forever, baby or no baby, this is all she wants now. To be present, to believe in magic again.

A Moral Question

Fred Johnston

It seems a fraud, this
To offer an opinion from a safe distance
Touching a flame
But pulling back – a game of sorts
Or worse, a fashion

A sticker on a car's rear window
Or wearing your *kaffiyeh* (but not too often,
It's not easy to keep clean)
Or signing one more petition
In the safe, safe high street –

And there's always an irate
Poem or letter to a newspaper –
They must be worth something
They must be worth *some*thing
And it's the thought that counts

Still an ache that the thought is weightless
You keep that notion at arm's length
We can only do what we can do
It's not entirely a waste of anger –
Or so you tell yourself

But you are not among the ruins
You are not swallowing tear-gas
Or making verses out of bandages
Nor composing to the rhythm of hammering
On your door

So you must wonder
By what right – it's a moral question –
You open yourself
To any of it. You run no risk.
You'd feel better, perhaps, if you did.

But then, and each time,
An itch, a nudge, a wink from the heart
And from this other far place you're
Putting new words in order
In spite of yourself. In spite of everything.

Biodiversity

Claire Hennessy

What you need is an intermediate disturbance.

One fallen tree in a forest
(let's not fret about its sound)
lets the sunlight in.
The plants in exile creep back,
breathe, fill up the space.
Decades later this patch
will win all the prizes for diversity.

You'll find hundreds of species
where coral reefs meet crashing waves,
where storm clouds sometimes loom,
and if anthozoans could talk
they'd spout fridge-magnet wisdom:
adversity makes you more resilient.

Like Goldilocks, nature demands it be just right.

Too small and there is no impact on the status quo.
Too large and a void cracks open,
a black spot where only the hardiest survive,
and that is not most of us.

Survival Games

Geraldine Mills

'TODAY'S THE DAY, BOYS,' Mam said. 'Hop to it.'

She was standing by the door, in her navy dress with polka dots. The sun was already coming up over Mike Carty's field. We looked at our schoolbags thrown on the floor; the homework we had fought over to get finished the night before so she would finally let us down to the Lallys'. We looked at her, at one another.

'But...'

'There'll be no *buts*.'

We knew the drill: to run around and shut her bedroom door, put the sign up 'Do not disturb' so that if Dad came home from the bookie's, he'd think Mam was sleeping and not wanting to make noise, he'd go out into the shed with his paper, checking the odds, hoping to pick out a winner this time.

We followed her along the path – hurried through the gate after her. Before we had worked our way into the next field, we heard the school bus coming over the hill. 'Down,' she cautioned, and we hunkered behind the wall, as silent as the stones. We heard it stop outside Lallys' house first, the swoosh of door as it opened and closed. Then its short journey till it pulled up at our gate, beeping three times before it gave up on us and took off again. When we knew it was well gone, we walked to the place where the field met the woods.

We sat under a shadowy beech tree like the one that had fallen in the storm, the one we helped Dad haul back to the house for firewood. Ticks dropped from the leaves onto our arms and we murdered them before they sucked any of our blood.

We were hungrier than any of those parasites, but Mam said that we had to learn. When the time came for the world to go belly-up, we had to be able to fend for ourselves. To survive.

Weak with hunger, we stripped briars of their purple-juiciness, scavenged hazel-nuts from the branches, cracked them stone against stone, and pulled out the sweet kernels. We wolfed any ghostly mushrooms that appeared from the earth like magic where the cows had been. We ate every bit we could find while our mother opened her bag, took out her mirror with the abalone shell on the back and started to shape her mouth as if she was about to meet the president or something.

Once we ate berries red as her lipstick and we puked all over the place.

'Boys. That'll learn ye,' she said.

A hawk circled above. She taught us to recognise that moment when the small bird realised it was in the claws of its fate, its curdling screech and feathers flying. A terror that no other sound equals.

'You watch closely,' she said through the red gash of her mouth. 'You watch until you can see no glint of life in the thrush's eye.'

We did as we were told, stared at the hawk standing on the stone wall. Its legs flexed over its prey, its imperious look daring anyone to take its dinner from it.

'Let that teach you not to let anyone ever, I mean ever, get close enough to dig their claws into you.'

The hawk lifted itself then, with the dead-meat in its claws. Flew back to where it came from.

We lived high in the sound of its squawking. Between ground and air. We were not twins, no not that, but living side by side, as if we were. The two of us nothing if not together. Always trying to make sense of her, especially the things she hated: fish, with eyes, on a plate, the smell of new books, snivilly children. The Lallys'. Always the Lallys'. She couldn't bear them. 'Jumped up snotteries,' she called them. We didn't know why she was so set against them, because we loved them, their warm, welcoming house. When she was in one of her 'gone days', and Dad wasn't down in the shed, we knew to run to them, and they'd let us in. They had three girls, older than us but they all dressed the same: Margaret, Lizabeth and Una. They always washed their hands before dinner, said grace before meals, asked to be excused from the table. We knocked at their door and when they opened it to us, the treadle on their sewing machine would be flying up and down, the whole kitchen filled with the scent of butterfly cakes: Lizabeth slicing the top off the buns, Una gluing each half with jam like they were wings, Margaret placing two each on our plates. What we loved most about them was that they never made small of us when we shoved the whole world of sweetness into our mouths.

Mam said we had to learn how to hide ourselves, to live below the earth if we wanted to be saved when the time came. She covered us over with moss and soil, strips of rotting bark. Dirt and crawlies got into our mouths, but we didn't cry because that was today's lesson. She said it was a small price to pay for not having our throats slashed or having to walk miles with bear skins on our back. We hunched under there until the quiet was too much for us. Coming out of hiding, our throats were still intact but slit by a hunger that was unbearable. She would be home already, as if we never existed.

The door was locked when we got back. Peering through the window, we could see her lying on the couch, the little grey blanket over her, the telly blaring. She had switched on *Judge Judy*. She loved that programme, the way a girlfriend was always suing an ex-boyfriend because he 'totalled' her truck or he slept with her mother or brother. Their spitting hate soothed her, lulled to sleep by it, like a baby would be hushed by a mother's voice.

We found Dad down in the shed and told him about the door being locked. 'You know your mother,' he said. But we didn't.

Without a word, he bundled us off to the bookie's with him. He made us stay in the car and brought us out a bottle of Coke, crisps and a Mars bar each. As soon as we had eaten it all we played the breathalyser game. Sticking a biro into the side of the empty crisp bag, we decided who would play the guard first. One of us stood outside at the driver's door, the other sat and wound down the window to be breathalysed. We took turns blowing into the bag. Whoever blew the most was the one over the limit and thrown into the jail of the back seat, singing *I'm in the jailhouse now*. When Dad came out and flittered his useless stubs into the ground, we knew there'd be no point in asking him for a choc-ice.

By the time we came back Mam was herself again, frying up onions to give the kitchen a lovely dinnery smell. But we had learned by now. Fried onions didn't mean dinner. Fried onions just meant fried onions.

Dad pulled chips from the freezer and chucked them into the oven. We dug into the food. Dad asked us about school. We lied. We always lied.

At night, after watching telly, we dreamed about hitching a ride in a truck crossing America. Find our own place. Shoot us a few coyotes that came too close to our ranch, hang their pelts on the gate to scare off the other critters.

If not that, then we'd move in with the Lallys until Dad came back from the bookie's. We sat at the kitchen window, watching the whole family go out in the car together, drive past our house, parents in the front, the three girls in the back, on their way to the pictures or the seaside. Lizabeth gave a little regal wave as they drove by. Even in the rain they went on picnics, telling us they had sat in the car at the beach, while their mother poured out hot chocolate from her flask, ate their ham sandwiches with no crusts, then searched out sea glass in the sand for their collection on the windowsill.

We finished our fried onions and oven chips and asked to be excused from the table.

'Where did you hear that?' Mam said, her face white with anger. She picked up the pair of us, dragged us down into the shed. Pushed us into the old sleeping bag Dad sometimes used down there. Then she hung us up from the big strong hook on the shed door. How she had the strength to lift us is anyone's guess. The dull twack of the hazel stick on the cloth when she walloped it. Twack, Twack. Saving us from the full sting of her beating. Feathers and dander in on top of us, sneezing. Afterwards she flopped us onto the ground. 'Let that be another lesson to you,' she said.

That last summer it rained all the time. Mam was gone a lot. We spent more time with the Lallys than at home. We sat on the lino of our neighbours' hall and Margaret showed us how to play cards. She taught us how to deal, to cut, how to create two bundles and with a quick phht, dovetail them like a flash into one another before placing the reshuffle in the centre of the floor. She taught us Beg O' My Neighbour, and for hours every day we played it, unaware of the rain gathering in puddles outside the door. Mrs Lally came in from the kitchen with a tray of Kimberley biscuits and Cidona in its brown bottle. The lino was warm and cosy from us all sitting there.

Mr Lally came to our door one evening to tell Dad that he had got a job up the country and that they'd be moving before school started back. We packed our school bags with our pyjamas, our toothbrushes, and the *Airfix* models they had given us at Christmas. We didn't bother with Mam's book on 'Survival Games', but we left a note for Dad to tell him we were gone. We stood at the side of the road while the removals men put the last of the crates into the back of the truck, clamped the door shut and drove away. Our neighbours' car followed after and when Mr Lally saw us he wound down his window. 'I'm sorry you can't come with us, there isn't enough room.'

His words drove our hearts underground, but we said we had other plans and were going to hitch a ride across America in one of them huge U-Hauls. Stop at a county fair, a rodeo maybe, watch them roping and branding, mutton-bustin'. Eat corndogs. Then we stuck our tongues out at them, waited until the car was a speck in the distance and Dad found us, took our bags and brought us back home.

The day the Lallys' postcard, with a round tower on it, fell through the letterbox, we found a wren's nest in a hole in the wall. Mam plucked out three eggs. She said she would give a prize to whichever of us could hold one of the tiny shells in our mouths the longest, then plopped one onto our tongues.

We sat there afraid to talk for fear of squashing them. We sat there until she didn't have hers anymore and she said it was time to go home. We forgot, let our teeth fall through the fragile shell, our mouths filled with its tiny moon of yolk and the breaking promise of feather and beak.

All we could think of was a birdie growing inside us and how it would fly out our mouths as soon as we opened them.

Geese

V.P. Loggins

Outside a racket as of geese in flight
pours through the gaps around the door,
    the windows, which face the walk

    where children from St. Mary's School
pass before my house in the waning light
    of December, the afternoon blown

    by wind through leafless trees that line
the chilled street, the children flying
    in twos and threes on their course

    across the neighbourhood to homes
where someone, I like to imagine, sets
    two cookies and a glass of milk

    on the kitchen table. As my mother did
when I was a child and before she slipped
    into the cold of a winter's leafless afternoon.

    I like to imagine the children landing like geese
in the cove of their parents' home where each
    and every one of them can paddle together

    or alone on the peaceful pond of permanence
where nothing and no one has yet been lost,
    and wind has not ruffled their feathers.

The Colour of You

Edel Hanley

One time I gathered leaves the colour of you between my palms, leaves the colour
of old oaks and Spanish chestnuts that had come loose during the first
storm that winter.

I thought of asking if you'd noticed how easily those leaves dissolved inside the auburn
glass of autumn that stirred beneath our feet as you went on and
walked toward the red,

birdless sky, professing how much you hate it when the hydrangeas brown this time of year,
every year, and how the dahlias grow frail and weak until they too turn
to die.

We go on talking like this until the conversation fades behind a crab apple and cinnamon
stick sunset and I stop to hear amber-skirted trees calling your name
as if it was my own.

Shadow Artists

Susan Rich

Out of the moon we weave borrowed wings
until we come to the greasy hours
and the cafeteria soon opens to the synagogue of
insomniacs who have spent all night
where schooners will not travel, where the heavy
clogs of nurses slap along over polished hallways.
One offers ice chips as if our father
were a frigatebird, adjust his tubes
against barnacled hands and sends us into morning.
We hoard *Cheerios* and onion rings, pile them high
on plastic trays, create a calligraphy out of chocolate syrup
along a bowl of oatmeal or perhaps mashed potatoes.
At the next table, tall waterfalls of tears
and behind us a family plays at baroque theatre.
It's 7 am and my sister's craving chicken wings,
a wax paper cup of Guinness. No one judges.
One slept, one eye in the water of waiting,
in the glasses clouded with fear, in the stink of
borax and bleach mixed with essential oils.
What are we doing here?
I look down at my doughnut, my Hawaiian shrimp.

What to call this place of the not living/the not dying,
waiting for the doctor's gospel, the nurse's falsetto cheer?
I sneak my dad a hot fudge sundae accompanied
by a half carafe of ginger beer. Around him
dream clouds lengthen.

The Witch

David Butler

THE HEGARTY PLACE WAS A HALF-MILE out the canal, between the lock and the humpbacked bridge. It was on the far side, which only had a rough path running along it. It wasn't what you'd call a house, either. More a couple of shacks thrown together slap-dash in a yard full of nettles and burdocks and an old bathtub. 'Before planning permission was a thing,' their da said. Joseph Donlon TD had been town councillor before he got into the Dáil on the third count. 'An oul sympathy vote,' Blinky Roche sneered, giving Joey a sneaky dig in the back. Because it was only a year after their mother died. Blinky Roche's da had been deselected by the party for openly criticising Mr Lemass.

Siobhán once asked their da how come such a monstrosity had been allowed in the first place. After that, Joey could never think of the Hegarty place without thinking of the word monstrosity. And the bloody mongrel that was kept chained to the gate was a right monster you'd want to steer well clear of any time you were passing there on your bike. At one time, there was meant to be a whole tribe of Hegarty children running wild out there. But now it was just Bridie Hegarty, living on her own with cats and hens and a goat. And that vicious oul tyke she kept chained to the gate. She looked like a red Indian squaw, face all wrinkled and smoky, hair a mad grey tangle. 'All her kids were taken off her by social services,' Siobhán said. 'And weren't they right,' said their Aunt Ciara, 'and her a dipso?'

It must be sad, though, to have all of your kids taken away.

There were all sorts of stories doing the rounds about Bridie Hegarty. How she was an oul witch who sowed ragwort in fields at night to poison the cattle. How she could make an animal miscarry by giving it the evil eye. How she drowned puppies in a rough sack. How she was arrested twice for drunk and disorderly, and once for scratching the policeman's face who was arresting her. But there were other stories. How she'd been a nurse over in England during the war. Then she'd come back afterwards with an English squaddie who had skin grafts and nightmares where he shouted out. It was that squaddie who'd knocked together the shacks out on old Dinny Hegarty's scrap of land out the canal. Then within the year he'd upped and left, though Titch Brennan said that wasn't true, and that Bridie Hegarty kept him chained up inside the shack to this day. Siobhán said that no-one knew who the fathers of Bridie Hegarty's kids were, only that every one of them had had a different father. Auntie Ciara clucked and made a sour face when she said that.

Siobhán was a Mount Anville girl now. Even before the bye-election, she'd made up her mind to go to boarding school up in Dublin. Joey could never get his head around why. He'd've sworn she was happy here, even after it was just the three of them. Or the four of them, counting Auntie Ciara who'd moved in to look after their mother when she was dying of cancer and then stayed on in the spare room. Auntie Ciara was a spinster. That was a funny word because it made Joey think of the skinny little spindle that was always spinning around on top of the Singer sewing machine she worked at every evening. But Ciara Donlon wasn't skinny. She was hefty and pious. His dad said that about her, even though she was his own flesh and blood.

Siobhán always seemed to be in flying form any weekend she came home, with her stories of high jinks in the dormitories, and eccentric nuns, and the films they got to watch every film night. 'It's a top school, Joey,' his father explained to him that first night on their own when he couldn't sleep because his gut was hollowed out and emptiness was like a fist jammed in his throat. 'Siobhán's the girl for getting ahead. You watch, and you learn, boy. With a good education behind her, there'll be no stopping her.' And sure enough, she'd come second in her class that year in the Inter cert. Though their da went spare when he saw the miniskirt and Beatle boots she wanted to go out in to celebrate.

It was a real gut-punch when Joey heard she wasn't going to be coming home for the mid-term. Siobhán always came home for Halloween. It was Siobhán who carved the pumpkin into a Jack o' Lantern and sliced up the barmbrack so each of them got something. And Siobhán organised the games their mam used to organise – ducking for sixpences, or trying to bite coins out of a hanging apple with your hands behind your back. The thrupenny-bit was the easiest because it had so many corners. It was Siobhán who'd taken him down to the huge big bonfire they always had on the green in the council estate. Every year they'd stack tyres and all sorts of rubbish for weeks beforehand, even though the guards were forever saying it was illegal.

Then a couple of weeks ago he'd overheard his da and Siobhán having a real shouting match on the phone. He was upstairs in his room and all he heard through the floorboards was his da's side. 'I will not stand by and have this family disgraced,' and 'If your poor mother was alive,' and 'Have you no thought for anyone but yourself?' And after that his da had been livid for days, barely speaking to him, Joey, though it was hardly his fault. And the upshot was, Siobhán wouldn't be coming home for Halloween this year. And to make matters worse their da would be staying over up in Dublin, too. On Dáil business, he said. So Joey was supposed to stay stuck in the house with Auntie Ciara for company.

So when Titch Brennan and Blinky Roche said they were planning a raid on the Hegarty place with bangers and sparklers and a couple of fireworks smuggled down from the North by Roche's da, and was he game for it, Joey said yeah. But all day it gave him a worry pain. And it wasn't because he was scared, either. It was because one day back in fourth class he was playing soldiers with Steven Madden down by the lock when Bridie Hegarty came along, wrapped up in that filthy coat she always wore that smelled of piss and was more a blanket with buttons than a coat. And Steven Madden, who was a bit of a daredevil, stood out in front of her and asked her straight out, 'What was it like during the war?'

She looked shocked to hear the question. She was too used to schoolkids sniggering and mocking and firing stones at her shack from the town side of the canal. And the upshot was, she brought Steven Madden in past the dog who just sniffed at him and on into her shack and when he returned he had a wooden box the squaddie must've left behind with medals and cap badges and bullet-cases and best of all an Iron Cross that he'd took off a dead Gerry. All that year, that box was their treasure chest in the secret den that even Siobhán didn't know about. But then Steven Madden's family moved away.

Titch Brennan said they weren't doing no cowardly long-range attack from the town side of the canal like the St Declan's boys. They were going all the way inside the compound so they were. There was a gap in the fence round the back where the mongrel couldn't see them and even if he could the chain wouldn't reach. They'd rendezvous at the lock at twenty hundred, and go in after dark. Then they'd make their getaway down the other direction to where the humpbacked bridge was.

Joey knew well he'd get into trouble. After tea Auntie Ciara said it was okay for him to go trick or treating, but not to go anywhere near the bonfire on the council estate and to be sure to be back home by eight o'clock. He was eleven, for God's sake! Besides, eight was no damn good. They were only meeting up at eight o'clock.

If his da had been home he'd never have dared stay out, that's for sure.

It was overcast, but it looked like the drizzle would hold off. They lay at the gap in the wire fence, all three of them, their faces darkened with mud like commandos. But first they needed a volunteer to do a recky. And since Joey hadn't brought any of the ammunition, Titch Brennan said it was down to him to go in. There was no electricity in the Hegarty place, but there must've been an oil-lamp lit because there was a buttery light glowing from the back window.

His heart hammering, Joey crawled through the gap in the fence. Twice he looked back at the four eyes that were peering after him from between the dock leaves. The sick yellow moon smouldering behind the clouds seemed to give those eyes a malevolent glimmer. There was a coal scuttle by the old bathtub. He hauled it over to the window, slowly so as not to let it clank. Then he carefully climbed onto it to have a look in.

Everything was blurred. It was as if the glass was sweating on the inside.

But there, sprawled on the kitchen table inside the window, he made out something absolutely crazy. It was shaped like a huge white letter M. But it was like the graffiti M scrawled up in the jacks that Blinky Roche had shown him and sniggered at. An M that was meant to be a pair of women's legs spread out knees up with her bits on show. And there on the kitchen table, through the blur, the feet of the M had stockings on and now he could make out the rest of the girl's body lying down flat on the table going away from him with the skirt thrown up over her tummy. And now at this end stooping between the stockinged feet, there was Bridie Hegarty's head, all bleary like it was underwater, but he knew it from the tangle of greasy hair that fell thick as brambles. But what was she doing? She had some sort of a plastic bottle or tube in her hand. And then the other person ,the one flat on the table, moved her head and seemed to look up straight at him and Jesus, oh Jesus Christ! Oh Jesus Christ!

The coal scuttle teetered and his leg slipped. He crashed over, upending it. At once the mongrel let out a torrent of barks and he heard the chain rattle and catch. And he was already scrambling for it.

He tumbled out over the fence and ran like crazy, ran away from the cascade of barking in the direction of the bridge this time, ran blindly, heart hammering and breath raw and eyes wobbly with tears and just when he got to the bridge he ran straight bang into his father.

Which was crazy because his father was up in Dublin.

But there was the TD's Hillman Minx parked in where you couldn't see it from the road and that was his da's heavy tweed overcoat he was grabbing hold of and burying his nose into. Joey looked up into the shocked white face and he cried, 'Da, she's got Siobhán, Da! We have to help her! She's got Siobhán inside there, Da!' but already the gloved hand was clamped tight over his mouth and his father's voice hissed, 'Would you shut up to fuck for Christ's sake, Joey.'

What Lies Ahead

Moya Roddy

For years a pair of barn owls
wintered in our garden –
once the cold set in they'd appear,
nest in one of the tall pines.
We came to recognise their tell-tale
shrieks – not the toowit toowoo
of fairytales – more the sound of an
animal in distress.

They seemed to tolerate us,
circling the garden at the edge of dusk,
light catching their feathers – until –
with a swerve of wings
they'd vanish over the rooftop –
leaving us to the creeping dark.

Blackout

Pat Mullan

I rode the New York subway that night just like every night.

My lifeline from Manhattan to the Bronx; oblivious of its clacks and clonks and its crush of human bodies, I trusted it to take me safely through. I watched my fellow passengers squeeze tighter together at every station, making room where there was none, hanging on to a space hard won, warily watching each new face that joined us as the doors slammed shut.

I rode the New York subway that night just like every night.

A squeamish stomach in the morning would never serve me well as I pushed into the garlic smell from those who'd eaten an alien meal, and I often guarded against an opportune feel. But in that very same milieu I learned a deeper lesson too, when a young man gave up a hard-earned seat to get a lady off her feet, or when I'd observe the unlikely reader, one with hard-worked hands, use chipped finger nails to turn the page.

I rode the New York subway that night just like every night.

At each new station the doors slid open to let some disembark and many others board and I'd watch the passing parade on the platform, strident, smart, sluggish, anxious, impatient, briefcases or bags, or nothing at all, newspaper clasped or open, or none at all, studiously avoiding each other, the body language of survival.

I rode the New York subway that night just like every night.

Sometimes the train would stop dead between stations without explanation and we'd wait in the stifling heat, silently suffering, sweating together, waiting patiently for a reprieve, always knowing that it would come, trusting that train to see us through before we succumbed to claustrophobia or lost our cool and blew it too; and then, that numbing feeling as we moved on, and the tunnel lights flashed by, hypnotizing us as we thundered through the ink-black tunnel.

I rode the New York subway that night just like every night.

Black Cat in the Garden

Liam Aungier

She is herself this lazy afternoon
Prowling through the jungle of your flowers,
Whose leaves are not greener than her eyes,
Nor the delicate rose more pink than her rough tongue.
Her tail, upright, brushes the wine-glass of a tulip.
She has no song but caterwauling, yet knows
In Egypt once her kind were worshipped, she
Who worships only the sun, enjoying now
Its brazen heat along the length of her back
Blacker than midnight among the yellow narcissi.
She claims Pangur Bán as antecedent,
She who gives without stint such gifts:
Her company, her coat so good to touch,
A dead robin on the doorstep of a morning.

Timing

Tina Morganella

HE TRIED TO EXTRACT LOVE FROM HER, quite against her will. Just like that – extract. Like a tooth. Because she resisted. She was surly and rude. She avoided eye contact and tittered coldly at his flirtations. She worked at the coffee shop. He bought coffee. He slid her a napkin with his name and phone number. She glanced at the too-thick black texta and crumpled it up immediately, tossing it into the bin while he stood in front of her. She stared at him until he walked away.

He was persistent, though. Stubborn but polite. He took up the challenge with gusto and patience. It became a game. A simple cappuccino, the napkin with his number. He kept sliding it across the counter. Sometimes, when he was feeling low, he turned and left to avoid the crushing rejection. Sometimes he smiled at her, then grinned ruefully at her dramatic crumpling, her narrowed eyes. Despite the clanging coffee machine, the whistling steam, the stern tap of cups on saucers, they both noticed the peculiar silence between them during these fraught exchanges. Sometimes his brown rainproof jacket squeaked. Sometimes she huffed, short and quick.

They never spoke, outside of 'Yes?' and 'A cappuccino, please.'

What kind of man could fall in love with a woman like that? One who was used to being rejected, but who also was never repelled or dejected by it. He nurtured a positive mindset – he courted rejection, he leaned into it. He vied for her attention regardless of the constant failure.

It's not that she didn't want to fall in love, it was just that she knew it was a bother. That it would tire and exhaust her, that it would extract energy from her like a blazing sun. And like the sun, she could be blinded by it, burnt. Taken to the extreme, she could be extinguished altogether. It had almost happened, once before.

Cappuccino. Napkin. She noticed his name was Tom.

Cappuccino. Napkin. He noticed that she had a freckle above her pinky knuckle, and that her earlobes were different shapes. He knew her name was Karla, from her nametag.

'Why don't you try a different coffee?' Karla asked him one day.

The napkin froze midway across the counter. He beamed. 'I'm a constant man.' He slid the napkin the rest of the way.

She smirked. Then she rolled her eyes while crushing the napkin.

Undaunted. Cappuccino. Napkin.

That complacent, patient expression.

'Stop!' she said angrily one day. It had been a particularly bad morning. 'Just stop it. You *fool*.' She ripped the napkin to shreds before throwing it in the bin.

He had the grace to blush. He spilled his coffee in his hurry to get out, a scar on his sweater.

He didn't go in for a couple of days. Karla scanned the morning queue on Wednesday. She bit her lip, frowning to herself.

Thursday, the corner of her mouth gave an involuntary tweak, almost a smile. But when he reached the counter, she quickly scowled instead. She said nothing.

Cappuccino. But no napkin.

They stared at each other a long moment. Then he nodded at her, once, turned on his heel and left.

He never went in again.

Karla sat outside on her break, one sunny Friday afternoon. She sat at a tiny circular table, the wrought iron tabletop leaving imprints on her arm. She propped open a paperback with her elbow, a coffee in one hand, and a cigarette in the other. As she blew smoke into the air, she saw Tom walking past.

'Hey. Cappuccino man.' She hadn't meant to say it aloud.

Tom's stride faltered. He'd never seen her outside of the shop.

'Hey.'

He had stopped but wondered if he should keep moving. He gave a small wave. Sunlight bounced off his watch into Karla's eyes.

'That's a nice watch.' It had a crisp white and silver face, and a smart black leather strap.

He smiled.

'May I?' He flicked his eyes at the chair beside her and rocked back on his heels once.

She shrugged. 'For one minute.'

He slid into the chair swiftly and hitched up his shirt and jacket sleeves to show her the watch more clearly. 'I made it myself. It took two years. I'm a watchmaker.'

She raised her eyebrows, her eyes wide. 'Huh! Really?' She was doubtful. Begrudging. 'It's nice. Classy.'

'The thing is, the inside of watches are far more beautiful than the outside. Let me show you.'

She butted out her cigarette and waited.

From his leather satchel, he took out a small suede pouch filled with slender metal implements held snug in their own satin hooks. 'My tools.' He grinned at her.

He took off his watch and laid it on top of a menu. Then taking one of the hooked rods, he carefully flicked the back panel off.

Gold. Pierced-out plates. Curlicues and flourishes. Intricately stacked disks. Sawtooth edges. Rubies the size of pinheads. Curved levers like cursive letters. Fine engraving, chased around the edges. The steady tick tock of time.

She was breathless for a moment. 'I've never seen the inside of a watch.'

They both leaned in closer.

'You made this?'

He smiled. 'Each teeny tiny piece.'

Such a small, inanimate creature, carrying the weight of time on its shoulders. A watchmaker must be a gentle man.

'You never know what lies beneath the surface of most things. That's the risk we take. Sometimes there's rust. Sometimes there's gold.' His steady gaze was obvious. But he was more confident now.

She pressed her lips together and nodded. Gave him a tight smile that might have been a grimace.

He carefully snapped the cover back onto the watch, then slid it onto his wrist. He stood up, hoisted his satchel over his shoulder.

'See you, Karla.'

'Tomorrow?' Her voice was little, crouched down in the back of her throat. She kept a finger hooked into the paperback still in front of her. Her other hand fluttered to her hair, tucked it behind an ear. Her gaze slid away from any eye contact.

'Sure.' His voice puffed out like the feathers of a parading bird.

The next morning, Tom ordered his cappuccino. He waved his credit card over the machine. He was respectfully silent. He didn't dare present his napkin. But when he reached out to take his cup, her fingers curled gently around his arm and he looked up, startled.

'Wait.' She couldn't smile. But she slid a napkin, marked with black texta, across the counter towards him. 'Here. Take it.'

Bright Poison

Carolyn Claire Mitchell

Empty fields scorched.
Fox kits flared from their den.
The frenetic exalted.
Soft, dark places
floodlit with certainty.

A brittle sort of light,
insisting on itself, refuses
that which holds it: holy
darkness - vast,
resplendent,
dauntless.

A wave denying the sea.
A tree denying the earth.

When that cold light cracks
What comes in?

Anemones

Jean Tuomey

Sometimes it's their white heads
waving in through the window
that remind me of my father.
He planted them
when I was too young to savour
their enhancement of our meals.
There may have been twenty, even thirty,
now spread to fifty, maybe a hundred.

Today, when my mother suggests
I bring some anemones back west,
how could I refuse? I don't have a window
like hers near my table, but wherever
their slender stems take root,
they will carry the flavour of home.

In Remembrance

Catherine Power Evans

I did a dirty thing in a graveyard
in broad daylight
with you.

Over cold shoulders of grey gravestones
sad angels knelt, watching.
Creeping mounds of moss shrouded the whos and whens
of clans from lands of granite hills.

Serpentine limbs writhed in slime
cast off a thousand worms, defiling desiccated bones
in a Celtic knot of lust.
Last-gasp clouds hovered amid the realms as we lay
between schist slab bed ends.

You cried milky tears as I corpsed
beneath the twisted yew.
You shuddered and the lone crow cawed
its scrawny call.

Daffodil

Nora Brennan

I was in my prime,
my body stretched to fullness,
my face radiant in the spring sun,
a halo of gold around me.

I did not expect to be struck down,
to collapse in the face of adversity.

It was early March.
Fluff and fur fell from the sky
like a magic carpet, covering
the grass pristine white.

I lost sight of my companions and feared
I would break under the burden.

Bent low, I kissed the ground
and hung on, a voice inside telling me
to stay close to the Source.
Thaw came. The drip, drip and spill.

I felt the warmth of sun on my back
and I began to respond, to lift myself up
and stand tall again. Among my own,
we were gathered as if in a choir,
our mouths open in song.

A Normal Woman

Eimear O'Callaghan

NORA HAD READ THE LATIN NAME OUT LOUD, going over the vowels that used to trip off her tongue, switching the syllables to be stressed or unstressed. Latin had been her best subject at school. *Levator palpebrae superioris*, a mouthful for the muscle that opened and shut her eyes.

Stress, the internet suggested, could be causing the violent twitches in her eyelid that made her vision flicker like a scene in an old silent movie, or too much caffeine. Alcohol too.

Levator palpebrae. She repeats the term to herself the next morning. She could contract the muscle even more and go on pretending she's asleep as his cloying new-day smells swamp the room. Shampoo and coal tar soap, whatever aftershave he has selected for the day. She slips her cheek along the pillow to a patch that is cooled by the breeze from the open window.

His footsteps crossing the stripped wood floor, clicking when he strides to the wardrobe, muffled when he walks on the rugs. She could tell him to shut the bathroom door and block out the thrum-thrum-thrum of the electric fan, but she won't do that.

'What the hell's that on your hand?'

Good morning to you too, my dear, she thinks of saying but doesn't. Without looking at her hand, she swipes a strand of hair off her face. Rosie who trims it every month insists it's ash blonde, but people have always told her lies. It has always been mouse-brown, fading now to grey.

Nora rolls onto her back and raises her hand above her face. September sunshine, spilling through the bathroom door, picks out the three black marks.

'I must've done it in my sleep. I don't remember.'

'Fuck's sake. That's all I need.'

Her eyelid twitches and she reaches for her glasses. There was a time when he never swore.

'What the hell is it?' he says. 'Somebody's name? Initials? What the …?'

Each letter is an inch high. 'I' and 'A' and 'D' etched diagonally across the back of her hand, from just above her wrist bone to the knuckle of her index finger. The rollerball pen that's usually in the drawer nestles between the pages of the book she'd been reading, a turned-down corner marking where her eyes had given up.

The bathroom fan drones on and Nora drops her arm, dead weight. Her tongue feels hot when she wets her finger on it, then rubs the letters into a bruise-like smudge. It will mark the sheet but she tucks her hand under the pillow anyway.

'I told you. I don't remember…'

'It's not as if you've much to remember.'

'A' for amnesia.

'I must've been dreaming. It's nothing.'

Nora seldom remembers her dreams. But sometimes, when she goes out walking and her breathing slows, an image flickers before her like a ripple in silk, a fish slithering out of her hands.

If you want to understand your dreams, she has read, start writing them down. She has never done it.

He stands by the window in front of the mirror and loops his navy tie, once, twice. He jerks the knot and cracks his collar into place.

'You're getting weirder,' he says, talking at the mirror and putting on his jacket. 'I've told you before. Your head's going.'

'I' for idiot.

Nora shuts her eyes as the fan cuts out and silence fills the room. He will lift his wallet from its resting place on the dressing-table and place it inside his breast pocket. He will check his tie once more. She won't release her breath until he has rapped his knuckles twice against the bed frame and clicked his way across the landing.

'Don't be doing anything stupid.'

———————————————

Leaves flutter along the avenues of oak and beech trees and gather in piles around genteel, detached houses like her own. On the main road, a snaking procession of traffic cones glints in the late morning sunshine. The traffic isn't moving but Nora isn't in any hurry.

Go, stop. Stop, go…

Even I could do that, she thinks, and waits for the man in a yellow high-viz vest to swivel his sign, granting her permission to move. Thirty years ago, when children were still a possibility, her husband had assured her that no wife of his would ever need to work.

Ignoring the stench of burning rubber, Nora rides the clutch. An elderly woman in a turquoise anorak steps off the pavement a short distance ahead and darts between the stalled vehicles, around the orange and white plastic cones.

Like their kingfisher, years ago. The flashes of colour and a sun-dappled riverbank, the distorted reflections of their feet in the cool, clear water. They'd gasped at the burst of turquoise, the blaze of orange and white, and clutched each other's hands.

Nora's eyelid twitches in the glare of the sun and she raises her fingertip to her temple but the black spots darting across her vision persist. She reaches for the sun visor, trying to ignore the dark shadows beneath her eyes.

What the hell…

The woman, wearing a white headscarf and barely taller than the bonnet, stares at Nora through the windscreen. Nora catches her breath as the door handle clunks.

Motorists to her right move off in the opposite direction. A young woman pushes a pram along the pavement. Two teenage boys batter each other with their schoolbags.

The old woman settles into the passenger seat, clutching a scrunched-up plastic bag, and the sign swings to 'go'. A horn blasts. Nora presses the accelerator as a van bears down on her in the rear-view mirror.

Keep on driving. Hold tight to the steering wheel. Nora drifts forward, propelled by the flow of traffic. Ten to two. That's what the instructor used to say. Hold the wheel at ten to two to keep a grip, to keep control. She grasps the wheel, resisting the car's urge to waltz to the camber of the newly laid tarmac.

'What's your name?', the old woman says, and smoothes the carrier bag across her lap. She clicks her seatbelt shut when the warning beeps.

Nora tells her and, tightening her grip on the steering wheel, manoeuvres between the rows of cones and past growling yellow diggers that claw and tear at the tarmac.

'What's yours?'

'Maisie.'

Or maybe she said Mary, perhaps even Mavis. Mary, Mavis, quite contrary, how does your garden...

'Where are you going?', the older woman says.

I'm going mad, she wants to say, I think I'm going mad. 'D' for doolally. Upended, skedaddled, like the plastic cone she'd clipped a moment ago.

'A meeting.'

It wasn't the time to admit that she was going nowhere and had nowhere to go.

'Where are you going?'

'The doctor,' the woman says and folds up her bag, squeezing out the pillows of air.

The old woman's stare hovers above the dashboard. She could bring her home and make her tea. Or she could stop and order her out. That's what he would do.

'What time's your appointment?' Nora asks.

'I don't know. Maybe they'll take me early.'

Rubbing her eye worsens the twitch but it disperses any tears. Nora rests her elbows on the worktop and leans in to watch the bowl of broccoli going around and around in the microwave. As he walks towards the table, Nora follows his reflection in the steamed-up glass door.

'You think I'm going mad,' she says, without turning around to face him.

'I didn't say that.'

You don't need to, she thinks, watching him in the spattered glass. He yanks off his tie and drapes it over the chair. Moments later, the cranking of the new lever corkscrew that he brought from the States, the gloop of a cork.

'You and your bloody dreams,' he says. 'Again. You're the one who needs a doctor. Not her.'

The seconds count down in digital green flashes. She should have told him nothing

'It wasn't a dream.'

He holds the bottle to his nose before filling their glasses. Nora lifts the cover from the broccoli and welcomes the balm of hot steam on her cheeks.

She scrunches her eyes. The *levator palpebrae superioris* mustn't let her down. He mustn't see her cry.

'You must've encouraged her, invited her in.'

'I didn't.'

The piece of cod that had glistened, almost translucent, on a bed of ice at the harbour sits dull and solid on their plates. Nora's homemade herb crust hasn't saved it from her efforts to keep it warm for him. She chews, trying not to gag, and fills her glass again. He pushes the bottle along the table.

'So, what the hell did you stop for?'

'I didn't. I didn't do anything.'

Nora starts as he slams his knife and fork and pushes away his plate.

'I can't eat this,' he says.

Nora holds the edge of her plate. The old woman had been so composed. 'What did you expect me to…?'

'Do? You mean, if it ever actually happened?'

The coffee drips on the tablecloth as he pours himself a cup.

'Did you report it?' he says. 'A pensioner in a headscarf hijacked you?'

'She didn't hijack me. She…'

'She's a phantom of your imagination. That's what she is. Or maybe one of your mother's blessed apparitions?'

He scrapes his chair back across the tiles and empties his coffee in the sink.

'You couldn't even dream it properly. A thug in a mask holding a gun to your head? Oh no. A little old lady with a plastic bag forced you to…'

'She didn't force me…'

'You're hallucinating. Again.'

Nora closes her eyes as his footsteps echo along the tiled hallway. 'D' for delirious, demented.

Once upon a time, she could have brought the woman home and he would have sorted it out.

'My little strange one,' he used to tease. 'The things that happen to you.' He'd take her to bed and kissing her afterwards would tell her she was odd.

'I can't take this anymore,' he says, returning with a coat over his arm. 'No wonder people are talking about you.'

But no one is talking about her, she knows that. Nobody talks to her anymore. The odd time a neighbour smiles, as if planning to stop, Nora quickens her pace and raises her hand, swatting an invisible fly. Her mouth gapes a silent apology. In a hurry, must dash. Something to do, somewhere to go. And she keeps on walking.

A fine dark hair, half an inch long, catches Nora's eye as she dips her arms in the suds. A single black hair, sprouting from her wrist bone. She turns her hands over and examines them under the light. A sign of madness when you're checking for hairs on the palms of your hands.

'I' for insanity.

She pinches the hair between her thumb and second finger and winces as she pulls it out.

She will lock the doors from now on, like they did when they lived in the city. It could have been a man with a gun. She could have been made to drive a bomb. She could have been kidnapped and held for ransom, her fingers or ears cut off and posted back to him. It had happened to people before.

In the early days, he would have paid a fortune, everything he had, to get her back.

'Things like that wouldn't happen to a normal woman,' he says, ramming the stopper into the wine bottle. He tells her not to wait up.

He doesn't need to tell her that he wouldn't have been so stupid as to stop. Of course not.

He would have had the doors locked. Of course, he would. Like any normal person.

Nora turns off the light in the stained-glass front porch and snibs the mahogany door. She slides the bolt in the door at the back.

He would have run the old woman down.

Appointment in Pottawatomie County

Jeffrey Alfier

Summer's handed the year its last warm evening.
I drove the hinterland, reached in little time the autumn

fields that edge the town of Shawnee.
Under a web of contrails, a farmer grinds a stubblefield to dust.

This year the maples shed early, parsing russet tones
among their deeper greens and the hunger-calls of crows.

Wind drags birds and brushfire smoke across my vision.
Ditches that line the fields are stitched to thorns.

Children pick through the small miracle
of blackberries. An aged couple

inured to the year's turning, sit in shallow light
under sweetgum and red oak that thinly shade

the deepscreen porch behind them. Wildflower holdouts
spin beneath the hooves of horses lathered in the cool air.

Footpaths curve blindly through bracken,
the sweet decay of overstory.

Sideroads cut so obliquely off the highway
they must have a need to lose themselves in unsaid secrets.

At the town's only diner, my waitress took her tip
without a word, her kindness having gone off the air.

Across the North Canadian River from here, a strip club's
set off by itself like a compass point, its dense-dim atmosphere

between votive candles and the candied scent of dancers.
I depart late, frost drawn tight on my windshield.

Sunday Afternoon at the Saltmarsh

Martina Dalton

Everything here is a reflection
of something else –
waiting for sun to break through.

Not knowing which section
of the marsh it will bless.
Light

spread thin as spilt milk.
Birds fall like breath – drawn
to some magnetic field.

Wet sand like icing not quite set
holds the prints they've made.
Beyond the bank

a golden place,
too far for me to walk today.
From this distance it looks

like the span can be swum.
First flies of summer
tumble down the windscreen.

Larks, a transistor radio
trying to tune itself in.
Mahler's *Adagietto* – on repeat.

Dwayne's Table

Dave Margoshes

Dwayne's a sociable fellow, hates
to be alone. He invites a bunch
of friends to join him at his table.
But Dwayne arrives a bit late, finds
his table full and winds up on his own
with a group of strangers at a table nearby,
musing at how alone one can be in a crowd.
When Dwayne's name is called, his friends
lift their glasses in his direction but there is
no companionable clinking. Afterwards, he
joins his friends at the bar but they're deep
into the rhythms of conversation already begun
and barely notice, and Dwayne has trouble
picking up the thread. He packs it in early, goes
home alone, the way he came. His friends close
the place, drink one final toast to Dwayne,
in absentia.

The Mistress

Beate Sigriddaughter

NOT WHAT ANY OF US EXPECTED, THAT'S FOR SURE.

I remember our first meeting. I was at Starbucks reading a magazine article about Frida Kahlo. It wasn't all that crowded. Nevertheless, she stopped at my table, something frothy in a mug in her hand.

'May I join you?'

'Sure,' I said.

'I'm Linda. Linda Thomas.'

'I know who you are.'

'Oh.'

Greg had pointed her out to me one day in the public library where we met at the circulation desk by chance. She was studying the bulletin board. Small, dark short curls, almost translucent porcelain skin. Ethereal somehow. He didn't call her over to introduce us. Lovely, I thought then with a quick pang of guilt. But not nearly as lovely as she was sitting across from me at Starbucks.

'I'm Melody.' I extended my hand. She hesitated a fraction of a moment, then she reached across the table to shake.

'If you already know who I am, then you probably also know why I want to talk to you,' she said.

'Yes. Greg.'

'You're beautiful,' she said breathily. 'So I can understand.'

I looked into her eyes, and I had goosebumps on my arms, on my ankles. I knew my life as I had known it would not be the same ever again. All of a sudden, we were in a lengthy and involved exchange of mutual admiration, which hasn't stopped to this day.

This day. She's moving in today. We haven't told him yet. That is to say, I haven't told him yet. I don't know how to do it. Somehow, I kept hoping he'd figure it out on his own. Instead, it's become my job to break the news. Well, okay, I did volunteer, though I regret that now. Seeing the discomfort in her eyes, though, what else could I do? Still, she'd be better qualified, no? She's known him longer. Better. Though I don't know about better. Thing is, he has to be told. Sooner or later. Preferably sooner. That's all there is to it.

He really was quite wonderful as a lover. Exciting. Uplifting. I had dreams of doing my precious artwork 24/7 with minimal interruptions because he'd be busy spending time with his wife and his career. No children, thank God. And from time to precious time, he'd be with me. He always brought me roses. We always made love. It always was delicious. But always amounted to once a week or every two weeks for a few hours. It didn't disturb my comfortable solitary life. I liked being part-time lover to a man committed to staying with his wife. It gave me this shining sense of being loved and noble both. Far be it from me to disrupt a marriage.

He told me right from the start he would never leave her. I readily bought into that, with just the tiniest ache in my heart, to be sure, especially when he'd keep harping on about his commitment to her, but I still got to maintain my illusion of being noble. He told me he loved her. She was fragile and not sexually inclined. But lovely. Well, he was wrong. She's neither fragile nor asexual, though he was spot on about the lovely part. I'd never been with a woman before. Neither had she. We had no trouble figuring it out.

What we haven't figured out yet is how to let him know. We definitely don't want a threesome. As far as we know, he's still under the impression that she's moving out as a trial separation to sort things out for herself. For which reason he hasn't been with me for weeks now, a few months actually, because he felt he needed to sort things out on the home front, mending fences and all that. This of course made it convenient for me to avoid the issue which now can no longer be avoided. I did ask him once on the telephone, what if those fences can't be mended? He shrugged it off, confident that he could fix everything, given a chance. That in itself didn't come as a huge surprise. It was typical for him to interpret the world in his favour.

This might sound like a comedy, but it isn't funny. It might sound like poetic justice, but it isn't that either. Maybe it's all for the best. Per Linda, he likes novelty. And we like each other. She cried when she told me one time that once she's gone, he probably won't even notice, though his ego might. The tears were not so much over him, but over how negligible she felt in this world. I hope I can keep making her feel important.

As for me, I have no idea how my artwork will fare with all this imminent commotion. Unlike Linda, I haven't lived with another person since sharing a dormitory room first semester in college. And now, instead of painting flowers and mermaids, I'm hanging a glass bead curtain in what is to be her room. She really is lovely.

Metamorphosis

Marian Kilcoyne

Between our two lives there is also the life of the cherry blossom.
                                        - Matsuo Bashō

The chant to cut you down grew loud, citing danger with every storm.
Too close, too wide, too deep at root. Unwieldy and wayward in your
guardian spread. She walked away ablaze from other people's needs
built on crassness and realism, the foes of creation.
That night she dreamed they took you down, scaring root from earth
leaving a hole so chasmic, the cosmos juddered while the birds
shrieked
and bobbed in disarray. Lying in a shroud of cherry blossom the dream
wended its way through her, specificity its horror fuel.
Wild with grief she lopped off an ear to numb the senses, stay the echo
of her animal howls. The keening lasted all night, loss her swamp, sly
devils her captors. Dawn, and a pearly flushed conch lay on the pillow
emitting a briny scent, twice removed from sea and sand.
She rose and sashayed out, sweeping fresh clay along the path,
descended down into the void, raised her arms to the sky and listened
with her conch ear, to the wind psalms that would sway her new
branches.

Morning Wear

Alwyn Marriage

When you died I kept the full-length
dressing gown you made and wore
each morning in your last ten years of life

the intensity of its rich red velvet
relieved by the white crocheted collar
that is now unravelling.

After twenty years of daily wear by you
and then by me, the power of its soft caress
on skin is undiminished

and each morning when I slip it over
waking nakedness, my body revels in
your motherly embrace.

Weathering

Kevin Graham

1.

Fog rolling in over the whin, drifting
like smoke or time. Beyond the blue-grey
blur the sea resolves itself, gnashing
with gusto, spitting into spray.
A voice travels the mindless whir
as if on loudspeaker turned down low,
so low it's barely audible. Something stirs
in the worldly mire. It's a blow
to lose someone you've known for so long
their company won't let go.
Fat drops hit your coat like tears
as if from the hurt, the whole wrong
of it easing its way through you,
seconds turning to minutes, then years.

2.

When it lifts nothing's the same.
The leaves are crisper, the fields more vast.
There is no one to turn to and blame,
no ghost to see or doubt to cast.

Only old farm machinery clarifying
among tufts of grass and white horses
grazing on the sudden dreaming
future. Somewhere windlasses
chime and there's a source of rich
gratitude. The boundaries of love
crystallise into gatepost and stone wall
wrought over a never-ending ditch.
It's both enough and never enough,
a flight of fancy and a fall.

Queen Anne's Lace

Helen Jenks

So when the time comes, and
both moth and mouse sit quietly
on the cobbled edge of a wild
moor-hen morning, let us walk
out together, hands clasped and
feet in stride, gathering that
which sighs and sombers over
the cluttered trundle of our
path, worsted and milk-boned,
bushels of carrot and ivory
woven and worn. *Even still,*
you say, *there is beauty here,*
pocketed with the others
and brought back to sit on
the bureau until dusk settles
and it turns time to wilt,
slowly, withering into
the addled grey of old age,
facing the truth of dying
as if it is the afterthought
of having lived at all.

Mighty

Siân Quill

MY NAME IS MUIREANN. My mother calls me Muireann the Mermaid. But I have no tail. I have two legs, just like you. But my skin is covered in scales. Scaly. Scabby. Flaky. Freaky. These are the names they call me in school. The names I hear. They might say worse ones behind my scaly back.

I am a good swimmer. I am strong and graceful in the water. Not so much on land. I have long strawberry blonde hair and my body is thin but my arms and legs can travel fast when I swim. The spotty teenage lifeguard in our local pool called my back stroke 'mighty'.

The problem is I can't swim in the local pool anymore. Children cry and mothers complain. 'Uggghh look at her poor skin', 'Is that contagious?' 'Don't touch her, just in case', 'Better not swap towels, you never know'. They say these things out loud as if I cannot hear them. Hello? I am right in front of you. Look. Me and my scaly skin in the turquoise swimsuit.

I Am Here.

In the showers, my mother raises her voice and speaks clearly so the children and mothers will understand: 'My daughter has psoriasis,' she says and she pronounces it slowly for them. Sore. Eyes. Us. 'It is a skin disorder. It is not contagious. Not at all. It's a condition, a bit like asthma actually, except you can see it. My daughter is beautiful. Your comments are not.'

And with that, she takes my hand and we leave the shower area and walk through the changing room. We go outside into the car park with our swimming bags. We are still wearing our dripping swimsuits and flip flops. It is freezing. In the car, our bottoms wet the seats. Mum tries to turn on the heating but she forgets it is broken. She wallops the steering wheel with her open hand. Her face is wet but I am not sure if that is swimming pool wet or salt water tears wet.

'We are going to go home and have hot chocolate,' she says. Like this is an important decision.

We do not go back to the local swimming pool.

Instead, every Sunday morning, Mum and I go swimming in the Irish Sea. Mermaids swim in the sea, Mum says. It is their natural habitat. The salt and seaweed is good for my psoriasis. Although it does sting when I get in. Especially if my psoriasis has been bleeding. It stings but then, as I swim, the cold of the Irish Sea stings even more. In a good way. It's a tingling mingle of stinginess and I love it. My legs feel like they are burning but my face cannot stop grinning. I run down the steps and jump straight in. My mother inches in, toe by toe, with little squeals emerging from her mouth. Sometimes, she curses under her breath. But once she's in, fully immersed, apart from her head, she too gets that frozen smile. The 'I can't bear this cold but gawd I love it' smile.

One Sunday, I get out of the sea and Mum is wrapped in her purple towel, laughing with two other women. One of them is handing Mum a cup of something hot. I can see the steam rising off it. Mum takes the green plastic cup and smiles even though she doesn't know the names of these women yet. As I dry myself, I listen to their chattiness. 'Go on, have a flapjack, go on, I made them this morning.' The other woman laughs: 'You big liar. Who do you think you are? Nigella? You bought them in Tesco so you did. Six for two euro.' The women giggle again, high pitch from the cold and the slagging. Mum joins in. She looks pretty when she laughs.

The hot drink is chocolate and the lady, who did or didn't make the flapjacks, offers me one but I refuse. I want it so badly but yet I say no. Mum guesses I'm being shy. 'This is my daughter, Muireann, she's my mermaid.' The ladies smile at me and say I have lovely hair. They debate whether the colour is strawberry blonde or caramel. I wonder what they think about my skin. They don't look. They don't ask. They don't mention it. Sometimes children say too much and adults say too little.

Since then, we meet the same women every Sunday. Mum chats and I am silent. But I like hearing their cosiness, their teasing, their laughter.

One wild and cold Sunday when the sea is full tide, I bring brownies I baked myself and the ladies ooh and aah over them, telling me what a good baker I am and how beautiful my hair is and how I am the best swimmer in the Irish Sea. Mum beams with pride. I do blush a little but I am not as embarrassed as I let on. I enjoy their compliments and their kindness. Just at that moment, I hear a terrified scream. A frantic mother is shouting and pointing at the sea. Her daughter, a girl half my size, is in trouble.

The little girl jumped off the rocks and she's in too deep. I run. I don't think. Or maybe I do think. Too much sometimes, Mum says. My body moves fast. I sprint. I jump. I swim. I am a mermaid. I can do this. I can save this girl. I hear the screaming and roaring from the shore. The girl's mother. My mother? If I drown, Mum will kill me. I plunge under the waves and swim with all my might. My open eyes are sore. I can't see her. I feel the panic rise in my belly. What am I doing? But no, there she is, limp and sinking.

I grab her. It's not how I imagined it. It's not like in the movies. She's small but heavy and I am pulling and dragging her and I can't breathe so I kick upwards but just as I open my mouth to gulp some air, a wave crashes over me and, in that split second, water pours down my throat. I want to vomit. We go under again and I see her terrified green eyes stare into mine. I am a mermaid, I tell myself. I have no fear. I am a mermaid. My scales will save me. My scales will save her. I kick hard to bring us up. But she is pulling me. Dragging me down.

It's getting darker. Down, down we go. Holding each other. Staring at each other.

She sinks. I sink.

I feel pressure on my arm and I am pulled up, up, up through the cloudy darkness. I see her green eyes. I see the grey sky. I gasp. I gasp. I don't remember any more.

When I open my eyes, my mother and the spotty lifeguard from the local pool are looking at me. I am wrapped in a tinfoil blanket. There is an ambulance, too much noise and too many people. Mum's lady friends are looking at me. Anxiously. One is holding the flask and the other is gripping my tub of brownies.

'Is she alive?' I splutter.

Mum nods and starts to cry.

'Don't you dare do that again,' she says, wiping her eyes and stroking my arm.

'Did I save her?' I ask.

'You saved her and Mark saved you,' Mum answers.

I look at the boy called Mark and make a promise in my head never to call him spotty again. He has a lovely smile. A lot of spots but a lovely smile.

'Hi,' he says. 'You're a good swimmer but you're not a lifeguard, you big eejit.'

I don't know what to say to that so I say nothing. Mum's swimmy friends give Mark and me a hot chocolate and one of my brownies each. A crying woman runs over and hugs me. Then she hugs Mark and then Mum. She tries to say 'thank you' but she only manages to mouth the words through her tears and then races back to the ambulance and her little girl.

Mark says he is teaching a lifeguard class at the local pool. He suggests I take the course.

'We don't go to the local pool anymore,' I say.

'Why not?' he asks.

'I have psoriasis,' I tell him.

'Oh. What's that?' he asks.

I show him my arms, my legs. Flaky. Scaly. Scabby. Freaky.

Mark asks if it is contagious and, for the first time ever, the question doesn't make me feel angry. Or sad. I tell him it's not. It's just something I have.

'You're grand so,' he says.

Mum and me look at each other and smile.

'The class is on Saturday mornings. Half nine. Don't be late.' Mark walks away, taking another brownie as he goes.

Mum puts her arm around me. We sit on the ground for a while looking out to sea.

'Let's go home,' she says.

Before we walk away, I look down into the Irish Sea. It's dark, murky and dangerous.

I want to learn to dive into its depths. I want to learn to breathe under its waves. I want to learn to save lives. I want to be a lifeguard.

My name is Muireann. I have psoriasis. I am not a mermaid. I am a mighty swimmer.

We're in it Together

Pete Mullineaux

Spider Man's inky shadow, Sherlock's Moriarty –
inner and outer demons to be mind-wrestled. Try
to run and I'm dark energy, dragging your soles
in nightmare mud; nemesis of self-doubt, vortex
sucking you down, a voice saying: *'No escape,
travel to the edges, I'll still be here...'*

We are like Siamese twins wrongly separated –
inevitably you'll have to face me; but no need
for a face-off, once you accept I'm merely part
of your alter-ego, mirror to your thoughts. Let
me travel the road with you, move in the same
direction, like a tandem bicycle. We can share
the work: freewheel a while – lift those furious
feet off the pedals...

Sun

Brian Kirk

Even as the weather goes to hell
we glory in the memory of heat.
Days when we left the house without a coat,
ignored whatever the world might have to sell,
boarded a bus and found ourselves in town
among the crowds, as if we had just stepped
out for a paper. These selfish moments shine,
reflect a careless time when no one or thing
could move us to be other than we were,
like rude Diogenes basking in the sun.

Grey Area

Nora Baker

'HAVE YOU EVER DECIDED TO TRY SOMETHING that you didn't think you'd like, and then been amazed at how much you liked it? That's how it was for me with this bubble-gum ice cream. When I saw its pale blue colour, I thought it would be too sickly-sweet for me, but I said I'd be adventurous and try it out, and it turns out it's actually quite good.'

'That's all very well,' I said. 'But mind you don't drip it all over the floor. This house has to be spick and span for its new owners.'

Leah stuck her tongue out at me in response.

I ignored this childishness and turned back to the moving boxes. My daughter was nearing thirty, but sometimes she acted as though she was fifteen. She had said that she was going to help me with clearing out things I didn't want to take to the new house, but since she'd arrived, all she'd done was eat junk, talk nonsense, and coo over toys and clothes we'd kept from her younger years.

When I turned back to her again, it seemed she'd finished her snack. She was holding a silk scarf the colour of the sea, and the way she was looking at it, you'd almost think she expected it to come to life in her hands and flow away.

'You used to love that scarf,' I said. 'Do you remember one year when you were in primary school, you begged me to let you leave it out in the garden overnight before St Brigid's Day? You were convinced that she was going to come in the middle of the night and bless it, so that it would stretch out into a long cloak.'

'I remember.' But she frowned. 'Except I remember it being green, not blue. I swear, I have such a clear memory of it in my head being green.'

'It's kind of a bluey-green,' I reasoned. I was about to return to my work when I thought I'd share with her something I'd read about the day before. 'Did you know that in some languages, they don't have separate words for blue and green? Sometimes their speakers can have trouble telling them apart.'

'That's ridiculous, Mom. That's like saying that an English-speaking person can't tell the difference between various shades of the same colour, just because we only use the one word to refer to most of them, most of the time. Of course we can *see* the difference. Take this, for example.' She ran her finger along the coloured stripe on the side of our old, oblong computer. 'I can obviously tell that there's more than one blue to see here, even without using words like 'azure', or 'navy', to describe them. Hey, does this thing still work, do you think?'

'It should,' I said, glad of the change in subject. There was only so much I could handle of her know-it-all attitude. 'Your father even had it connected to the broadband there a few years ago. I had forgotten we even had it, if I'm being honest. There's probably all sorts of stuff on there.'

'Amazing!' Leah squealed, sitting down at the desk and starting to tap away on the dusty keyboard. 'Although it'll be strange to use it without hearing that creaky dial-up tone. I remember when I was really small, it used to make me jump, but now thinking of it makes me a bit nostalgic.'

I decided to leave her at it. If she was busy herself, it meant she'd have less time to distract me. Every now and then I'd hear a gasp or a giggle as she clicked on documents and photos that hadn't been opened for over a decade.

'This is like doing archival research on your own life! I found an Irish essay I must have written around 2004, about a girl called Gormla. Lots of *go tobanns* and *nathanna cainte* sprinkled throughout. Hilarious. Oh, Mom, do you think the webcam still works?'

'I don't know,' I sighed. 'Try turning it on and you'll find out.'

The next time I looked over, her face was glowing in the camera's blue light.

'I have got to video call my friends and tell them about this. They will *die* when they hear that I'm talking to them from this relic.'

'Suit yourself,' I said. 'I'm taking this stack of things to the kitchen. When you're done, would you mind taking the time to fill a crate or two?'

Carrying those boxes was heavy work. When I set them down in the corridor, I noticed I was sweating a little. I switched the kettle on for myself, knowing I would need coffee to get through the afternoon. From the spare room, I could hear Leah shrieking something about her 'self from the past'. I rolled my eyes, about to pour the water, when I realised that her voice didn't sound excited anymore. It sounded distressed.

I was trying to process this when she burst into the kitchen.

'Mom, Mom! You have to come. You have to help me. There's a me on the screen, but it's not me. It's not *now* me. It's an earlier me. It doesn't make sense.'

'Calm down, Leah. What do you mean? Did you find a video of yourself from when you were a child, or something?'

She just shook her head, tears welling up now.

In the spare room, on the old computer screen, I could see four squares on a camera call. Three of those squares showed the faces of Leah's friends, all looking bemused. The fourth square showed the empty desk chair where she had just been sitting.

'I think your friends are wondering what's going on, Leah. Why don't you sit down and talk to them?'

She wouldn't budge from where she was by the door, almost cowering.

I sighed and made my way over to the machine so I could terminate the call and give my daughter a talking-to. Then I noticed, when I sat down, that my image wasn't being picked up and transmitted on-screen. Or – my image was, but not as it should have been. The computer wasn't showing me in the chair, at the desk, in the spare room. In my little square of the screen, I was in my bed, stretching and yawning, wearing the pyjamas I'd had on the previous night. The me on-screen checked my phone and swung my legs out of the bed.

I waved at the webcam, hoping that the me on-screen would correspond, match my movement in some way, but I didn't. My body wouldn't mirror its own actions. In my video square, I padded out of my room in my pink slippers and started making breakfast. Eggs on toast, just like I had every Wednesday. Just like I'd had a few hours earlier.

The light of the webcam was still on, burning blue into my irises. Leah's friends were looking concerned, mouthing something, but they all seemed normal, sitting down and dressed like they usually would be at this hour, rather than going about their morning routine. One of them typed in the chat to ask what was going on.

'Is this a trick? Because it isn't funny, Leah. I don't know how you got this footage of me, but I want this to stop, right now.'

Leah shook her head again, still sobbing. 'It showed me... It showed me this morning. I was with Tony and we had a fight, and that's why I thought I'd come here and help you out with the packing. To take my mind off things.

But it showed me – it wouldn't show me now, it was showing me back then. At the start of the day.'

I turned back to the screen, where I was brushing my teeth, about to step out of my dressing gown and into the shower. Leah's friends were now looking embarrassed. One of them logged off.

'Maybe it's cursed.'

'There's no such thing as a curse,' I said, as firmly as I could, and I bent forward to plug out the computer. Mercifully, the webcam light snapped off. But I still felt uncomfortable in front of the screen, even though it was now blank.

'Leah,' I said. 'Pass me that box over there. The big one. I think it's time we took a trip to the dump.'

We loaded the machine into the boot of my Corvette and the car felt heavy the whole journey long, knowing it was back there. When we arrived at our destination, Leah murmured something about fly-tipping, but she dutifully helped me cart the box over to the least-grubby pile and leave it there. When we got back in the car, I doused our skin with hand sanitiser.

'I've just thought of something,' she said, when we were five miles down the road. 'Maybe the problem was with my account. Or maybe it was only with the webcam, and not the computer itself. There were nice things on there, too. Good memories, and creative stuff.'

I gritted my teeth but said nothing.

'Do you think that maybe... we've thrown away the wrong thing?'

'Leah,' I said, trying to stay calm. 'You can feel free to delete your video account as well, if you want to. But I am not driving back there to get that computer. I don't care if that's irrational. I am not going back.'

I looked over at her for a second. She was sullen.

'Is that clear?'

She nodded.

'Let's listen to the radio,' I said, when we were closer to our house and the adrenaline rush was starting to die down. I twisted the dial with one hand, but all I could get were blurry frequencies.

'Let me do it.'

I felt a shock of static as Leah pushed my hand out of the way. She twiddled around until she picked up the faint sound of a woman speaking. She turned up the volume.

'Is this a trick? Because it isn't funny, Leah,' I heard my voice say. But the words weren't coming from my throat, not this time. They were coming from the car's speakers, and I could hear Leah's sobs in the background. Our voices were distant, distorted, but still unmistakeable. We looked at each other for a second, eyes wide as we listened to ourselves from earlier. Then I snapped the radio off.

We drove on in silence.

Old Man

Forester McClatchey

Lying in bed till the ache settles way down in my joints, getting up with the birds, having nothing to do, gnawing the day to a nub, calling my daughter at dusk, receiving a jolt in the heart from the grown woman's voice telling me with icy formality to leave a message please, sitting on the porch and listening to the insects nibble leaves, wanting someone to call me, an insurance salesman, Jehovah's Witness, anybody, settling down in the dusk with a book I will never read, rising to answer my petulant bladder, sitting on the toilet with tears of effort, attending to the silence closing in around my castle of nerves, preparing for a long siege, feeling the rams and catapults hammer my outer walls to ruins and creak toward my keep, going to bed, lying in the dark, rising at the witching hour to piss again, contemplating the proper function of sphincters, falling asleep on the toilet on a cold night, waking ill, coughing, succumbing to a common sickness, worsening, peeling dried mucus from my chapped nose, sleeping for two days, waking in a world of white and tubes, watching odourless angels glide and bend and ask my name, forgetting that name, forgetting all names, forgetting everything but thirst, trying to ask for water, failing to secure the words, tiring of human company, rebuking a strange wiry woman for calling me Daddy, asking to be left alone, asking for water, not getting water, devils sitting on my chest, eyes making reddish clouds like kicked mud, coughing forever, imagining a cool squirt of water, coughing, lowering the core of me into nubbly blackness, feeling it lisp over me like villi, hearing muffled voices through the wooden lid, one person weeping halfheartedly, a bored voice muddling through scripture, the roar of the earth around me, the thump of confused voles, hearing the first wet scratch of worms on the side of the box, hesitant, polite, unsure, like a voice outside a room, saying, 'I hate to disturb you, but…'

First Death

Heather Laird

I WAS TEN WHEN MY GRANDMOTHER DIED. Not the nice one in the powder blue suit and matching hat who came on the bus for short visits with an electric blanket under one arm and a cooked chicken in her handbag. The other one. The one I grew up with. More to be admired than loved. At some point towards the end, I sent my mother down to the kitchen to make herself a cup of tea, insisting that I sit vigil on my own. I could claim that this was prompted by concern for my mother, the sole carer of my grandmother, but I remember my motives as largely selfish. I was the youngest in the family and desperate to catch up. Sitting with the dying seemed such a grown-up occupation that I was sure it would speed my transition to adulthood, or at least convince others of my maturity. Alone with my grandmother, however, I forgot all of that. Everything stopped except for her breathing, which I found myself focusing intently on. It seemed such hard work. So laboured. I didn't know how she kept doing it, but then again she had always been a hard worker.

My earliest memory of my father's mother is of her standing next to me in the bathroom, showing me how to fold and unfold one sheet of toilet paper so that it would suffice for all relevant bodily functions. Frugality a necessity perhaps when you marry a man capable of turning one of the best fields on a small Roscommon farm into a tennis court for the entertainment of him and his friends. The cast iron roller was still there when we were young and a favoured plaything, and a framed black and white photograph on the landing wall featured a number of men and women in old-fashioned tennis whites holding rackets, but the tennis court was once again a field. It maintained a sporting connection, however; when free of grazing cattle, its flattened surface made it ideal for family kickabouts on warm summer evenings.

My grandfather, who died long before I was born, was in danger of losing the farm when a mutual acquaintance put him in touch with a woman from the next town over who had just returned from America with twenty years' worth of savings and no husband. Neither of them was getting any younger, as the saying goes, so that was that. It sounds very transactional and though it's possible for love to come later in such arrangements, I doubt that happened in their case.

Part of the deal was that my grandfather convert from Methodism to my grandmother's religion: Anglican or, more specially, Church of Ireland. I'm not sure if that bothered him much, but the farm itself had strong associations with the Methodist movement; John Wesley had even stayed and preached there on a proselytising tour of Ireland, referring to my family in one of his journals as especially pious and God-fearing. A bible signed by Wesley had been proudly passed down through the generations until it was stolen by a group of American Methodists who asked to see it when they called to the farm as part of a bus tour of Ireland that followed in Wesley's footsteps. When my brother recently undertook a conversion of his own, turning the remains of the old house that had hosted Wesley into a party venue for his youngest daughter's 21st – complete with cocktail bar, a surround sound speaker system and strobe lights – my mother jokingly suggested that we go to the disused cemetery up the road and check the family plot for signs of turning in graves. I picture the inhabitants of that old house as a dour lot not much given to frivolous activities, closer in temperament and convictions to my no-nonsense grandmother than their spendthrift descendant. They certainly would have understood and appreciated my grandmother's extreme response upon discovering my siblings and I huddled around a candle at the kitchen table during a power outage playing poker for pennies.

Soon after the wedding, my grandfather confessed to having recently sold land to pay debts. The farm was no longer the size it had been when my grandmother agreed to marry him. She later recalled to my mother, walking the floor boards at night, considering her options. In the end, she bought the land back with some of her own money and kept it in her name. She then set about knocking my grandfather into shape and getting the farm back up and running. When the townies came calling, looking to play tennis with Georgie, she ran them; her husband was busy, she said. Her first encounter with these men and women suggests the extent to which they, and possibly her own husband, had underestimated her and the impact that she would have on life on the farm. They came knocking in their tennis whites and barely spoke to her when she opened the door to them, she told my mother years later, instead holding out their coats and umbrellas for her to hang up as if she were a newly-employed servant of the house. Did they look down on her because she had been unmarried until her late thirties and then, in their view, only managed to acquire a husband by buying one? Never one to question her own worth, she stood in the doorway with her arms tightly folded until they were forced to beat a retreat down the garden path, their coats and umbrellas still awkwardly held before them. The Boss, that's how your granny was known in these parts, an elderly pub-owner told me when I was in his bar at the age of thirteen or fourteen drinking pints of cider with my own townie friends and he asked me my name. I don't know how successful she was at getting her husband to do some work about the place – my mother says that he was an easy-going man even in her day – but my memory of my grandmother is that she was always on the go and liked to keep those around her active too. As soon as my siblings and I could walk, we were expected to help out on the farm. Collecting eggs, picking fruit and feeding calves were amongst our first jobs. We then graduated to washing creamery cans, milking cows and bailing hay. Keeping up appearances was also very important for my grandmother; flowerbeds and garden paths had to be weeded regularly and the brasses on the front door had to shine.

On her ninetieth birthday, my grandmother took to the bed. She was still fairly sprightly so I can only assume that it was a decision rather than a necessity. Perhaps she had simply determined that ninety was an appropriate age to down tools. Never one to do things by halves, she went from fully mobile to bedridden in one day. She had a bell by her bedside that she rang at regular intervals. My mother was tied to the house, tied to her, and with the aid of the bell she reigned from the bed as she had from the kitchen before. One day I decided to take vengeance on this elderly woman for the subjugation of my mother. I had a recently-discovered talent: I could meow just like a cat. I tiptoed to her bedroom door and meowed loudly. She rang the bell and I tiptoed away. I then came noisily down the landing. 'Are you okay, Granny? Do you need anything?' 'One of the cats has got into the house,' she said. We never had house cats, only feral ones that lived in the outhouses that I would occasionally try to tame. My greatest success was with the one that looked like it had a touch of Siamese; after sustained effort on my part, it not only allowed me to pet it, but would tolerate sitting on my shoulder while I proudly strode around the back yard. But even if tamed, my grandmother would not have welcomed cats into the house. She was a woman who liked clear delineations of the Victorian variety. Weeds had no place in a flower garden, animals lived outside and children respected their elders. I thumped around the landing, making a show of opening doors and looking around corners. 'Are you sure, Granny? I can't find a cat and I've looked everywhere.' Ten minutes later I was back, meowing outside the bedroom door. Again she rang the bell, and again I looked for the cat. When it was clear that she was starting to doubt herself and question either her hearing or sanity, or both, I stopped. Gaslighting, I think it's now called. My mother is nearing ninety herself and I only recently told her about my childhood act of retaliation on her behalf. She professed to being horrified but I didn't believe her; I could see she was struggling not to laugh.

In those final hours, I found myself matching my breaths to my grandmother's but could only sustain this for a brief period. The effort involved was exhausting. If it was so difficult for me to breathe in this way, what must it be like for her, I wondered. She could stop now, I gently told her. 'It's okay, Granny,' I said, 'you don't need to keep going. There's nothing more to be done. You can stop now.' I repeated these words and similar ones like a mantra, over and over again. I didn't know if I was doing right. I still don't. But it felt right, and her breathing eased, became less frequent, less laboured. The day of the funeral, I overheard my mother tell someone that she now regretted leaving me alone with my dying grandmother; she had deteriorated rapidly whilst I was sitting with her, my mother said, and I was too young to understand what was happening. But that wasn't how it was at all.

Detritus

Denise O'Hagan

From the Latin detritus (n), from deterere, meaning 'a wearing away' (from de-, 'away', and terere, 'to rub or wear'). Figuratively, it is used to indicate debris, or waste material.

From the pages of Maigret, another mystery – half a
letter, Dear J—, a stranger's cursive folded familiarity

a set of heavy polished silverware, swaddled in crimson
velvet, when every meal-time was an ornate occasion

a glass jar of foreign coins, pocketed kings and queens
pressed up to heads of state, circular edges of situations

a recipe for a neighbour's cake for Easter (Sambuca
underlined) pencilled onto April in a calendar of 1974

a drawer full of the secret lives of diaries, scribblings
of years shared, mostly; the steady dribble of days

bus tickets, library stubs, postcards repurposed before
repurposing became the thing to do, mini bookmarks

a typewriter lugged from room to room, its vowels
fingertip-faded, and a carriage return that still sticks

a small vase of HB pencils, office biros, and a gold-
nibbed fountain pen, when writing was a physical act

a drawstring bag of black polish, brush and well-
oiled rags; even in the wheelchair, his shoes shone

and slipped down behind the filing cabinet, her
last X-ray, curved and shelved in its own dust.

The Man Who Swam to Black Head

Stephen Shields

My uncle's woollen togs sagged.
'A man swam to Black Head,' he said.
He pointed beyond the beach, beyond
the sea, but I could not find a black head.
People gathered in groups upon the sand;
matrons in flowered swimming hats
did the Deadman's Float; some men
plied the water with a hesitant crawl.
Further out, his bald head glinting like
a fish, the man who swam to Black Head
ignored the crowd and frolicked
among the octopi, the jellyfish;
I thought I saw a walrus.

A Broken Phone Box on Clanbrassil Street

Gerard Smyth

Wires hang like dreadlocks from a Rastafarian's head.
This is a vault of breath, of tear-stained words
and sugary words now hushed between *Hello* and *Goodbye*.
In the time allowed rumour followed hearsay,
a voice could harmonise with a voice from far away.
Calls were made to save a life, seek forgiveness,
confess to shame or sometimes send a cry for help
that never came. The book of numbers has been torn,
flitters of it blow into the street.
The stuttering tongue said *Please come home*.
The voice in a rage shouted *Never return*.
Remorse and regret had their own libretto
in the phone box on Clanbrassil Street.
Once-in-a-while it rang and somebody passing answered,
asking *Who is this, where are you calling from?*
That mystery voice is out there, somewhere, still holding on.

Warriors of the Playground

Gargi Mehra

TYRES, ROLLS, FLOATS, LIFEBUOYS – our men find new and inventive words to christen the layer around our waists.

But the skinny mother at the playground flushes our species down a whirlpool. What sorcery does she wield to freeze the flesh of her upper arms? Why don't they jiggle when she cups her mouth and cries out to her toddler? How dare she parade her low-rise jeans and crop top? Why don't her breasts bounce when she tumbles behind her tot and grabs his bike seat so he doesn't keel over?

Why don't our moans ever cease when a torrent of cheese melts upon our tongues?

The waif fiddles on her smartphone. Her boy juggles a football on his knee, or tries to. Some of us cluck our tongues. The others shake their heads – how fledgling moms these days let their cubs roam free. They never glance up and away from their private little bubble.

But not us. We secure our cherubs. A few of us helicopter them while the rest trade handy one-pot recipes. When the minders grow tired, duties are swapped. The recipe-hoarders chase the kids, while the others strike up gossip.

The seconds tick past. We paw the ground, drool dribbling from the corners of our mouths, our eyes bloodshot, thirsting for the needle of disaster to prick the bubble of bliss.

Calamity would strip away the layer of contentment – it always did. Our brats plunged into accidents even before we snapped to our senses. Every one of us had braved the trauma – freezing on the spot when a tot wailed, decoding if the tenor and pitch carried our helix strands, rushing to our tot and kissing their scrape, and hurrying home to slap mercurochrome on the wound, all while they sirened in the background.

The skinny mom's boy swoops into a seat on the swing. We suck in our collective breath. The boy has blazed through four summers of life – what else can injury do but hunt down him and his joints?

Time floats past.

He propels himself like a human catapult, and stumbles. Some of us witness the exact moment he slides off the seat and flies through the air for a moment before landing on soft grass.

He runs bawling to his mom. Metal hits wood as the waif sets down her phone. She scoops him into her arms. We count the seconds until her meltdown. Someone unleashes a heartfelt 'aww', but the rest of us stare her down.

The boy's bawling attains fever pitch. Tears dance down his face.

Reams of skin flash before our eyes. Buttons snap open, shirt shrugged out of, bra lowered. The boy latches on like a magnet, his mouth the South Pole to his mother's true north. His moans taper off, the gift of life fastening his lips shut.

Some of us gasp, hands flying up to cover mouths. Others recoil, and rock back on their heels.

Who among us has nursed a toddler? We scan the faces of our companions, seeking a culprit, a guilty party, a mother who ran the marathon we coveted to win.

A few of us drop our gazes. Now everyone knows.

We watch. And wait. The boy's head disappears into the cloth of his mother's top. Her hand rests on his cheek, the tips of her fingers running through his hair.

We squirm in our spots. We shift our weight, pressuring the earth from one foot and then the other.

The cherubs on the playground squeal, and sprint across the grass.

The latch breaks. The boy's mouth unclasps from his mother's core. She relieves us of shame by veiling her assets.

Some of us grab our little mites and drag them home.

Others settle on the benches. A packet of Dorito's switches hands. Low guttural growls of hunger issue from the core of our being, but we slap our own fingers away.

What does the skinny mother's husband nickname her stomach? Washboard, floppy disc, mousepad, post-it, pancake.

Bog Oak Finale

Patrick Devaney

This bog grows richer from neglect,
Bright with pink-flowered willow-herb,
Shady with thriving sally trees,
Mantled with long-stemmed grasses.

A whinchat chatters from a branch,
Swallows twitter overhead,
And by a rusting horse plough
A moist frog rustles in the sedge.

When I was young a neighbour
Arriving here in early May
To strip and cut a turf bank
Used rouse us with his belling song.

And by that gap my father once
Angrily opposed a man
Who wished to cart his turf clamps
Out across our meadow field.

Behind those cypress trees
My mother often toiled alone,
Planting lettuces or spreading sheets
To bleach on tussocks in the sun...

Today there is no person near –
A tractor visits once a week –
And that thought makes me realise
That nature by itself is not enough.

Last year beyond that smothered drain
An ancient trunk of dried bog oak
Stood like a human carved from jet:
A grass fire burned it down –
This year the grass grew back.

The Crannóg Questionnaire

Patrick Chapman

How would you introduce yourself as a writer to those who may not know you?

I'm a writer of poems, fiction and scripts, but my main occupation has always been poetry. This began because of a misapprehension – starting out I thought it took longer to write a story than a poem, so I went for the easier option. Little did I know. My books now include eight poetry collections and four books of fiction. Plus, during the first year of the pandemic, I wrote a non-fiction book about the films of David Cronenberg. What better way of distracting oneself from a viral outbreak? My next poetry collection, *The Following Year*, will appear in 2023 from Salmon.

When did you start writing?

When I was about seven I had the impulse to write a book, so I got my hands on some tourism leaflets and copied them into a journal. The next attempt was more original; at about nine years old I started writing stories and illustrating them. Later, a teacher allowed me to write stories instead of essays, and he would correct them. Poetry came later still, quite by mistake.

Do you have a writing routine?

I don't have a regular writing routine. When I'm working on a poem it sits in my head until it's either finished or abandoned. A few of the pieces in my previous collection, *Open Season on the Moon*, arrived when I rediscovered abandoned drafts I'd completely forgotten about, from 1992. They proved useful compost material in which to grow new works. Other pieces have been done and dusted in half an hour, so it varies. If I have a deadline, my routine is one that many writers may find familiar. Panic, write, despair, write, panic, write, submit, despair. But not always in that order.

When you write, do you picture somehow a potential audience or do you just write?

I don't think of who might read the work. Each piece tends to guide me towards the shape it wants to be. One useful trick is to pretend that no one will ever read it. That way I don't have to worry about what anyone will think, which can be liberating, especially during the initial phase of composition.

Some writers describe themselves as planners, while others plunge right in to the writing. Would you consider yourself a planner or a plunger?

I'm a plunger, definitely. I throw up whatever comes out, then see what's there. After that, the organisation begins. I'm a fan of the 'open-mode, closed-mode' way of working. Editing is always enjoyable, as it allows me to be ruthless with whoever-the-hell wrote this stuff, i.e. me, earlier. Planning can enter the process when it's time to clear up the potent mess of the first draft.

How important are names to you in your books? Do you choose the names based on liking the way they sound or for the meaning? Do you have any name-choosing resources you recommend?

In my stories, names tend to arrive as I write and they either stay as they are, or change as intuition requires. They're not consciously designed to reflect the character. I do admire authors who give their characters appropriate names. Winston Smith, Binx Bolling, Holly Golightly, Patrick Bateman. (An aside: at an event years ago, Bret Easton Ellis asked to whom he should sign my copy of *American Psycho*, and when I told him my name, he did a double-take.)

Is there a certain type of scene that's harder for you to write than others? Love? Action? Erotic?
They are all hard. Love scenes in general are to be avoided because they're so open to bathos, the male gaze, technical inaccuracy, societal displeasure, and pregnancy.

Tell us a bit about your non-literary work experience, please.
I worked in advertising as a copywriter but the pandemic means that I'm a full-time poet now. As well as that, I'm co-editor and designer of a poetry magazine, *The Pickled Body*.

What do you like to read in your free time?
Recently I read Philip Pullman's marvellous allegory *The Good Man Jesus and the Scoundrel Christ*, which is an insightful examination of how revolutions are corrupted by those who seek to gain from the sacrifice of others. There's a pile of science-fiction on my to-read list, as well as the new Claire Keegan, and a non-fiction book about the Lockhart plot. Occasionally, I dip in to Patrick Horgan's marvellous readings of the Sherlock Holmes stories. Every so often I pick up a poetry collection and read it from cover to cover; sometimes I go back to old favourites, such as Kate Clanchy's *Newborn* or Thom Gunn's *The Man with Night Sweats*.

What one book do you wish you had written?
I Am Legend by Richard Matheson. It's beautiful, extraordinary and so influential. One day, someone will make a film that does justice to this story but none of the adaptations so far has managed it.

Do you see writing short stories as practice for writing novels?
Writing short stories is practice for writing short stories. It can help with honing one's prose skills, but a novel is a different beast.

Do you think writers have a social role to play in society or is their role solely artistic?

Writers have no obligation to play a social role in society but are as entitled as anyone else to do so. In terms of the work, some of the most important pieces of art have been made from a creative expression of outrage or a need to warn of danger. *Guernica* is an obvious example. *1984* is another. Art and writing can also have unintended political effects. Who knew that 'We Will Rock You' by Queen would be taken up as a protest anthem? So, in short, whether a writer plays a social role or is solely artistic, depends on the writer, and the response to their work – which is something they have no control over once the piece is out there in the wild.

Tell us something about your latest publication, please.

Out in 2023 from Salmon, *The Following Year* is a poetry collection written during the pandemic but not because of it. Some of the poems are direct reactions to the state of the world in the last year or two; others go deep into memory and deal with how someone evolves out of the larval stage of depression into a sort of rueful clarity. My atheism provides the inspiration for some of these poems. There is also a lot of humour that some would call dark.

Can writing be taught?

Writing can be taught, in the sense that space can be provided for writers to teach themselves by doing. The need to write is something that comes from within.

Have you given or attended creative writing workshops and if you have, share your experiences a bit, please.

Creative writing workshops have been crucial to my development. The first I attended was given by Eavan Boland during the summer and autumn of 1989. It was open to members of the public, applicants selected based on work submitted. Other participants included Conor O'Callaghan, Vona Groarke, Jean O'Brien, Noel Monahan and others. Not a bad crop. Eavan was a wonderful teacher: honest and helpful. When she gave us homework – write a villanelle – I didn't know what that was until she offered 'Do Not Go Gentle Into That Good Night' as an example. After the workshop, Eavan edited an anthology we put together, *Trinity Workshop Poets 1*. Her support for beginners is legendary, and I was lucky enough to have benefited from her teaching.

Flash fiction: how driven is the popularity of this form by social media like Twitter and its word limits? Do you see Twitter as somehow leading to shorter fiction?

I love flash fiction, and enjoy regularly checking it out at places such as *Splonk*. Like poetry, a flash piece has to pack a lot in, and its resonance can last a lot longer than its initial impact. That said, social media such as Twitter have reduced attention spans; shorter fiction is crafted to fit, and competition is intense – not just from other stories, but from all other distractions. A shorter piece may therefore offer a brief holiday from the apocalypse.

Finally, what question do you wish that someone would ask about your writing, and how would you answer it?

Q. How could you work in advertising as well as writing poetry? Aren't they antithetical?

A. Strange though it may seem, they enriched each other. Advertising taught me economy of expression. This fed into the poems: if at all possible, don't bore the audience.

Artist's Statement

Cover image: *Flora*, by Pamela Sztybel

Pamela Sztybel was born in New York City in 1956. She received an undergraduate degree from The New School University and an MFA in Painting from the New York Academy of Art.

In addition she has won fellowships to the Santa Fe Art Institute with Wolf Kahn, the Vermont Studio Center and the Scuola Internazionale di Grafica in Venice, Italy. She has served as a board member of the Vermont Studio Center and on the Art Collection Committee of The New School University.

Sztybel has participated as a visiting artist at the American Academy in Rome and as a teacher at the Scuola Internazionale di Grafica. She has also taught workshops and lectured at Claremont Graduate University, Connecticut College, West Liberty State College, Long Beach Island Foundation for the Arts, and The Huntington Library and Gardens in Pasadena.

She has had solo and group shows at Spanierman Gallery in NY and Easthampton, Wickiser Gallery in NY, Southern Vermont Arts Center, The Committee in Los Angeles, Jill Newhouse Gallery in New York, Southampton Arts Center and the Washington Art Association.

She has illustrated 'Little Known Facts About Well-Known People' by Barbara Guggenheim.

Her work also appears in *American Tonalism* by David Cleveland.

Her paintings can be found in the Art in Embassies/US Dept. of State as well as numerous private and corporate collections.

Follow her on Instagram at Pamela Sztybel.

Biographical Details

Jeffrey Alfier's most recent book, *The Shadow Field*, was published by Louisiana Literature Journal & Press (2020). He is co-editor of *San Pedro River Review*.

Liam Aungier has had poems in *The Irish Times*, *Poetry Ireland Review* and previously in *Crannóg*. A first collection, *Apples in Winter*, was published by Doghouse.

Nora Baker completed a Bachelor of Arts with Creative Writing at NUI Galway in 2017. She is currently a graduate student in French Literature at Oxford University. She has been published in an anthology by Small Leaf Press, and is working on an Irish-language novel.

Nora Brennan's poems have been published in various magazines including *Skylight 47*, *The Kilkenny Poetry Broadsheet*, *Crannóg* and *The Stony Thursday Book*. She was awarded Second Prize in the 2019 Jonathan Swift Creative Writing Awards, Poetry Section. Her first collection of poems, *The Greening of Stubble Ground*, was published in 2017. She was a mentee in the Words Ireland National Mentoring Programme 2020.

David Butler's third novel, *City of Dis* (New Island), was shortlisted for the Kerry Group Irish Novel of the Year, 2015. His second short story collection *Fugitive* (Arlen House) and third poetry collection *Liffey Sequence* (Doire Press) were both published in 2021. Prizes for the short story include the Fish International, ITT/Redline, Maria Edgeworth (twice) and Benedict Kiely awards.

Martina Dalton's poems have been published in *Poetry Ireland Review*, *The Irish Times*, *The Stinging Fly*, *The Stony Thursday Book*, *Crannóg*, *Skylight 47*, *Channel*, *The Honest Ulsterman*, *The Waxed Lemon*, and the Dedalus Press anthology *Local Wonders*. She was selected for the Words Ireland National Mentoring Programme 2019. She received a notable mention in the Cúirt New Writing Prize 2020 and was shortlisted for the Julian Lennon Prize for Poetry 2021. She won third prize in the Red Line Book Festival Poetry Competition 2021 and won second prize in the Waterford Poetry Prize 2021. She was awarded a Dedalus Press mentorship in 2021.

Patrick Devaney's poems have appeared in *Revival*, *The Galway Review*, *Boyne Berries*, *The Stony Thursday Book*, *Crannóg* and other magazines. He has published eight novels, including *Through the Gate of Ivory*, *Romancing Charlotte* (written under the pen name Colin Scott), and *The Grey Knight: A Story of Love in Troubled Times*.

Kevin Graham's pamphlet *First Impressions* with Ragpicker Poetry came out in November 2021.

Edel Hanley is researching for a PhD in women's war writing at University College Cork. She was awarded an Irish Research Council Postgraduate Award for her research in October 2020. She hosts poetry and short story writing courses for gifted children alongside the Centre for Talented Youth Ireland (CTYI) and her poetry and fiction have previously been published in *Crannóg*, *Skylight 47*, *Drawn to the Light Press*, *Aigne*, and *Quarryman Literary Journal*.

Claire Hennessy is a writer from Dublin.

Helen Jenks lives in Dublin and is the founder and editor-in-chief of The Madrigal Press. Her work has appeared or is forthcoming in journals such as *Green Ink Poetry*, *Spellbinder*, and *Dreich*.

Fred Johnston was born in Belfast in 1951. His most recent collection of poems is *Rogue States* (Salmon, 2019.) In 2020, he received an Arts Council Literature Bursary to complete a collection of short stories. Individual poems have appeared in *The New Statesman*, *The Financial Times*, *The Guardian*, *The Spectator*, *The Irish Times*, *Temenos Academy Review*, *Cyphers* and *The New Hibernia Review*, among others.

Marian Kilcoyne is an Irish writer based on the west coast of Ireland. Her poetry has been published widely in Europe, the UK, the US and elsewhere. Her book *The Heart Uncut* was published in October 2020 by Wordsonthestreet Galway. She is working on her second collection under the working title *False Face & Fascist*.

Brian Kirk has published a poetry collection *After the Fall* (Salmon Poetry, 2017) and a short fiction chapbook *It's Not Me, It's You* (Southword Editions, 2019). His poem *Birthday* won the Irish Book Awards Poem of the Year, 2018. www.briankirkwriter.com.

Heather Laird is a lecturer in English at University College Cork. She is the author of a number of scholarly publications, including *Subversive Law in Ireland, 1879–1920* (2005) and *Commemoration* (2018), and recently started writing creatively. In 2021 she was shortlisted for the MMCF Writing Competition (flash fiction category) and published in *Elsewhere: A Journal of Place*.

V.P. Loggins has published poems in *Poet Lore*, *Poetry Ireland Review*, *The Southern Review*, and others. He is the author of *The Wild Severance* (2021), winner of the Bright Hill Press Poetry Competition, *The Green Cup* (2017), winner of the Cider Press Review Editors' Prize, and *The Fourth Paradise* (Main Street Rag, 2010). The author of two books on Shakespeare, he has taught at several institutions, including Purdue University and the United States Naval Academy. www.vploggins.com.

Aoibheann McCann's work has been anthologised by Pankhurst Press (UK), New Binary Press, Prospero (IT), Doire and Arlen House. She has been shortlisted/placed in the *WOW*, Cúirt, Colm Tóibín, Maria Edgeworth and Sunday Business Post/Penguin Ireland competitions. *Marina*, her first novel, was published in 2018 by Wordsonthestreet. She is currently working on an audio comedy.

Forester McClatchey's work appears in *Plough*, *The Hopkins Review*, and *Birmingham Poetry Review*, among other journals.

Dave Margoshes has published six books of poetry, including *Dimensions of an Orchard* (Black Moss Books), which won the Anne Szumigalski Poetry Award at the 2010 Saskatchewan Book Awards. His most recent title, *A Calendar of Reckoning*, came out in 2018 from Coteau Books.

Alwyn Marriage's twelve books include poetry, fiction and non-fiction – most recently *The Elder Race* (novel) and *Pandora's Pandemic* (poetry). Her new collection, *Possibly a Pomegranate*, will be published in spring 2022. She is very widely published in magazines, anthologies and online, and has given readings all over Britain and Europe and in Australia and New Zealand. Formerly a university philosophy lecturer and CEO of two international literacy and literature NGOs, she's currently managing editor of Oversteps Books and a research fellow at Surrey University. www.marriages.me.uk/alwyn.

Gargi Mehra's short fiction and essays have appeared in numerous literary magazines online and in print. She blogs at gargimehra.com or can be reached on Twitter: @gargimehra or on Instagram: https://www.instagram.com/gargi_mehra/

Geraldine Mills is the author of five collections of poetry, three of short stories and a children's novel. She is the recipient of many awards including the Hennessy New Irish Writer Award, three Arts Council Bursaries and a Patrick and Katherine Kavanagh Fellowship. Her second children's novel, *Orchard*, was published in December 2021.

Carolyn Claire Mitchell lives and writes in Co. Mayo. She has had work published in *Poetry Ireland Review* and in *The Stony Thursday Book*.

Tina Morganella's short fiction, personal essays and travel literature have appeared in *STORGY Magazine* (UK), *Tulpa Magazine* (Australia), *Sky Island Journal* (US), *Entropy* (US), *Sudo* (Australia), *Litro* (UK/US), *Fly on the Wall Press* (UK), and the 2021 Newcastle Short Story Award Anthology (Australia), amongst others. She also has had nonfiction work published in the Australian press: *The Big Issue*, *The Australian*, *The Adelaide Advertiser*, and is co-editor of a self-published anthology of true stories about dating during COVID, called *Wear a Mask, Cupid!*

Pat Mullan is a thriller writer, poet, and artist. He is a member of International Thriller Writers. His novels, poetry, and short stories are published in the US, Ireland, and the UK. You can visit him at: http://www.patmullan.com

Pete Mullineaux lives in Galway where he teaches global issues in schools through drama and creative writing. His four collections include *How to Bake a Planet* (Salmon 2016). A new collection is forthcoming in 2022. His poetry has been discussed on RTÉ's *Arena* programme and featured on the *Poetry Programme*'s podcast *Words Lightly Spoken. Poetry Ireland Review* said of his work: 'Taut and razor-sharp, probing, beautifully written… a gem'.

Eimear O'Callaghan began writing short fiction in 2016 after a career in journalism. She won the 2018 Cúirt International New Writing Prize and Kinsale Literary Festival's Short Story Competition, Words by Water, in 2017. She was a runner-up in the 2021 Seán Ó Faoláin Short Story Competition and her work has been shortlisted or placed in several other contests. She is the author of *Belfast Days: A 1972 Teenage Diary* (Merrion Press, 2014) and is a former BBC and RTÉ journalist.

Denise O'Hagan is an editor and poet, and former Poetry Editor for Australia/NZ for *The Blue Nib*. With a background in commercial book publishing in London and Sydney, she set up her own imprint, Black Quill Press, in 2015 to assist independent authors. Winner of the Dalkey Poetry Prize (2020), her work appears in many journals, including *The Copperfield Review, The Ekphrastic Review, Books Ireland, Eureka Street* and *Not Very Quiet*. Her website is https://denise-ohagan.com.

Catherine Power Evans has been published in *Crannóg, Silver Apples* and *RTÉ* (collaborations), among others. Her short stories have been long-listed in the Colm Tóibín Short Story Competition and *The Stinging Fly*.

Siân Quill is a TV scriptwriter who writes for RTÉ's popular soap opera *Fair City*. She also writes for children's TV: *Becca's Bunch, Little Roy, Jessy & Nessy*, and has worked as a theatre actress. She was selected by the Irish Writers Centre in 2017 as a Novel Fair finalist. Her poem *Mosaic* was part of the Greystones Poetry Trail, 2020. She wrote and read a personal piece, *Goodbye to Renting*, on RTÉ Radio 1's *Sunday Miscellany* in May 2021.

Susan Rich is the author of five books of poetry, most recently *Gallery of Postcards and Maps: New and Selected Poems*, Salmon Poetry. She also co-edited the anthology *The Strangest of Theatres: Poets Crossing Borders*. Her awards include a PEN USA Award, a Fulbright Fellowship, and a Times Literary Supplement Award. Her poems have appeared in the *Antioch Review, Crannóg, New England Review*, and *World Literature Today*.

Moya Roddy's debut collection *Out of the Ordinary* was shortlisted for the Strong/Shine Award. She's been shortlisted for the Hennessy Award and her poetry has appeared in *The Irish Times, Stinging Fly, Boyne Berries* and *Crannóg* among others. Her recent novel *A Wiser Girl* (Wordsonthestreet, 2020) was described in *The Irish Times* as a 'blast of Italian sunshine, a sparkling glass of wine for these chilly times'. Her latest work is a collection of working-class stories – *Fire in my Head* (Culture Matters, 2021).

Stephen Shields lives in Loughrea. He writes poetry and prose. His work has been published widely in journals in Ireland and the UK.

Beate Sigriddaughter lives in Silver City, New Mexico (Land of Enchantment), USA, where she was poet laureate from 2017 to 2019. Her latest collections are prose poems *Kaleidoscope* (Cholla Needles, May 2021) and short stories *Dona Nobis Pacem* (Unsolicited Press, December 2021). http://www.sigriddaughter.net

Gerard Smyth is a poet, critic and journalist. His poetry has appeared widely in journals in Ireland, Britain and the United States as well as in translation. He has published ten collections, including *The Sundays of Eternity* (Dedalus Press, 2020) and *The Fullness of Time: New and Selected Poems* (Dedalus, 2010).

Jean Tuomey has been published in several journals. Her chapbook *Swept Back* was commended in Fools for Poetry 2018 and received special commendation in Blue Nib Chapbook 37, 2019. She is shortlisted in many competitions and came 2nd in Fish poetry competition 2011 and 1st in the Jonathan Swift Creative Awards for poetry in 2021. A former teacher, she trained as a writing facilitator with the National Association for Poetry Therapy in the US.

Stay in touch with
Crannóg
@
www.crannogmagazine.com

Lightning Source UK Ltd.
Milton Keynes UK
UKHW051629200522
403286UK00010B/179